Tell

The Next Generation

A.R. Michaels

~ 1 ~

First paperback edition April 2020

Book design by Tevin Cordom

Book Formatted by A. Cordom

Proofreading by Jonathan Cordom

ISBN 978-99916-966-1-4 (paperback)

For Any inquires, Contact Me At:
avrilrcordom@gmail.com

To My Children: Tevin and Kaylah
and
All the Cousins: Micaela and Diego, Jordan and Decan,
Tristan and Annie, Kiara, Keegan-Daniel and Kristopher,

Aunty loves you all. You bring joy into my life.

TABLE OF CONTENT

CONTENTS

Foreword

I want to congratulate Avril for an outstanding piece of work. Every teenager to elderly needs to get a copy. I was truly captivated and inspired as I discovered in the pages a fresh look on a very familiar portion of the bible, Psalm 28. If you decide to read it in 8 days, fasten your seat belt, enjoy the journey and act on every truth you encounter along the way.

Patrick Britz, Ekklesia Community, Walvis Bay

The book is awesome. I love it. It's inspiring, motivating and teaches you so much more than you thought you knew. I saw Rehab in a different light and her meaning or important role she played and how God blessed her to have a direct relationship to Jesus. I cried, I was so overwhelmed when Asaph was fetched and Carren broke loose and ran back.

This book is for the curious ones, the ones who dare to break loose and explore, go against society and all their previous beliefs and set foundations in honour of God. They are the ones to find the treasures... God's love and being set free from bondage. May God touch all supernaturally who reads this book and dare to explore, learn and accept all The Bible has to offer. I know children's' lives would be touched and changed at a young age with this book.

Sonette Abrahams

Introduction

Lost in the forest

Carren from the most beautiful town of Finelando, was a free spirit. She loved nature and always wondered into it, as it gave her the calmness and peace she longed, especially after the passing of her grandfather whom she loved dearly.

He was her, 'Pa'. Her best friend and companion and when she came from school, he would spoil her with a glass of the most delicious fruit juice, his own home-made recipe.

Today she felt different, it was almost as though she was called to the forest. Their house, relatively close and her parents always warned her about the psycho of the forest.

Rumours had it that he was older than all the people around and didn't get old. Those who apparently saw him made up their own stories. Others were fortunate to run away and some mysteriously disappeared. But as long as she can remember, no one had ever disappeared.

She's not afraid of nature, she loved the beauty around her when alone. And today the singing birds all contributed to the harmony around her.

She drove to her favourite spot in the forest, hid her bicycle beneath some overgrowth and took the footpath to continue her walk.

Her heart felt happy and joyful, almost in expectancy of something great about to happen. She strolled and admired the beautiful tall green trees and here and there a sunbeam shone through. She thought of asking her dad, to build her a tree house out here, but she knew it would not be permitted.

She trailed deeper into the forest, without realising she had reached the end of the hiking trail. Time stopped as she was too intrigued in her own thoughts. She looked up, and realised with a shock she had walked too deep into the forest, as the path in front of her was unfamiliar.

Panic gripped her heart as she struggled to breathe. Think Carren, think, there was no time for panic. Use the sun to find your direction home. She was familiar with sunrise and sunset and from there she would find her way back home. She tried hard to figure it out, but it seemed as though nothing worked her way today.

She tried to look past the dense trees, but the sun was blocked. She moved around now desperate to get from the forest. But time after time she took a wrong turn. She hit her foot against a stone and stumbled forward. She tried to prevent her fall, but it was too late.

When Carren came to her senses, she was surprise as she realised she fell through a hedge. What she saw on the other side, surprised her. A super bright light blinded her for a moment. Fear gripped her heart. Where was she? Then she felt something licked her face and a yell trailed the forest.

Where was she? What licked her face? And why the bright light? Her eyes got used to the bright light an then she laid eyes on the most adorable white fluffy puppy. It sort of reminded her of a Maltese, but it was slightly different. It continued licking her face and its tail wagged all the time, an indication that it was happy. Without thinking her hands encircled the puppy. Perhaps it was lost and together they would find their way home.

Her eyes now used to the bright light, looked around to familiarise her with the place. Her heart started to beat faster, as she saw and old man on a rocky chair looking straight at her. Was this the psycho of the forest she was warned about?

She froze in her steps, starring straight at the stranger. She knew she should get away from here, but the smile on the old man's face reminded her of her late grand-pa. With the puppy in her arms, she decided to walk up to him. She was lost and needed a way out.

She looked around for any other life, but didn't see any.

Asaph, sat on his cottage stoop and stared at the girl. He sent a little prayer, "Please, let she be the one. I've been waiting here for decades."

What Carren saw, amazed her. She had never seen a place like this before. Green trees, covered with flowers in various colours, ranging from pink, yellow, white, red – her eyes couldn't describe its beauty. She was left in awe with what she saw.

The old man got up, but by now her mind told her to run, but her feet kept moving forward.

As she neared the white cottage that looked like any other, just very old she felt a peace that surpasses her own understanding. Was this a magical garden? She locked the stranger's eyes and it was filled with love, if that was the correct word to describe his eyes. With his white grey hair and full beard, he looked like a biblical character in her storybook.

Slowly she climbed the old rundown stairs and on the last step she hesitantly decided to stay put.

A warm smile curved his mouth as his eyes shone love and it drew her near. She felt home and knew this stranger wouldn't harm her. He looked at her intensely and called her child.

'Child, what brought you out so far into the forest?' It can be dangerous to wonder out so far alone.'

The gentleness in his voice made Carren look into his eyes again, and she knew he couldn't be the psycho of the forest and wondered if he stayed alone.

He held out his hand, 'Asaph is the name.' It was almost as though he read her mind and answered, 'I am living alone, but never feel lonely. Missy keeps me company and here's a lot of gardening to do, so I avail my time with it."

Carren's eyes were drawn to a thick book. She could see it was very old and the book was evident that it had been read a lot.

The old man followed her eyes and answered with a smile, 'The book is what kept me sane over the years. You are the first visitor in many years."

A warmth overwhelmed Carren and she walked up to stretch her hand, 'Carren."

She wanted to tell him all will be okay, things will work out, but she kept quiet. She felt such a pity towards him and for a brief moment forgot she was lost. She wanted to know more about him as he reminded her so much of her grandpa.

She saw his eyes turned to the book again, and asked him the type of stories he loved reading and what his favourite one was.

Asaph smiled and replied, "There are more than you can count, and I love them all."

A beautiful white flower outlined with yellow fell from a tree onto her arm and slipped to the floor. She bent down and picked it up, held it towards Asaph, as she noticed the beauty of the overhang above her head for the first time.

Breathless she whispered, 'it's so beautiful. Did you plant them?"

"No, I found them here. These trees were always part of this little haven of mine."

Carren confused asked if someone stayed here before.

"No, but if you would like to hear where it came from, I would love to share the story."

Carren gave him a smile and said, "Okay, I'll listen to your story but then you should show me the way home."

The old man smiled and agreed. Typical youngsters, something for something.

He lifted the book and opened it right at the beginning and put it down. Then he stretched his hands and it was almost as though a screen appeared. She looked puzzled, but before she could say anything a realistic darkness appeared in front of her. Then she saw almost as though some spirit hovered over it.

Surprised at what happened in front of her, she heard a deep but gentle, loving voice. "Let there be light." The deep dark formless mass disappeared and light appeared.

Asaph moved his hands again, almost as though operating a smart interactive whiteboard. The voice continued, "I'll call this light, 'day' and the darkness 'night', for it to be morning and evening.

Carren was speechless as to what played off in front of her. It seemed like high tech, but she couldn't see any whiteboard. The display was great. She was hooked to hear more, but when she looked up, she knew she had to leave, as the sun was setting.

Asaph, looked intensely at her and he wanted to ask if she would come visit again, but he knew if her parents knew where she was, they would never allow her to come again. He knew the rumours going about him.

She looked as Asaph and took the old man's hands, "I am intrigued of what just happened, but I must go home. I know I didn't listen to your entire story, but I'll come back. I promise."

Asaph's eyes lit and a happiness filled his heart. One look at Carren and he knew she would keep her word. 'Carren, I'll be waiting for you. Missy will guide you. She knows the way."

Carren thanked him and took one last look over her shoulder and felt a warmth embracing her heart. She wanted to come back, but she also knew it might be the last time her feet would ever take this path.

Carren picked her bicycle and ride home. But the entire ride she was fascinated about what happened there. It was different there - peaceful and filled with love. If only she could visit the old man daily. What she saw and heard was so real, she wanted more of it, but knew it was just wishful thinking. She cannot go back to a strangers' little cottage. Or should she? She could take her cousins, Yaya and Noe along. They love the forest.

Carren couldn't wait for school the next day. She will convince them to go along.

Day 1: The Creation

The School Janitor Eavesdropping

At school, Carren couldn't wait for break time or perhaps even before school. The two of them usually hang together during break.

Carren rode her bicycle to school, as do most of the children. As she got to school, she was just in time to get a glimpse of Yaya. She knew her cousin too well, and her secret of the old man in the forest would be safe with her, as Yaya also loved stories. When the families visit, Yaya would be all ears.

"Hi, Yaya." Carren greeted as she parked her bike next to Yaya's.

Yaya's face lit up when she saw Carren, as she knew her cousin too well. If she tried to catch up with her before school there was something she wanted to share. "Out with it Carren, what's news?"

Carren looked around as though afraid someone might overhear and answered, "Did you ever wonder where day and night come from?" Yaya was quick to respond. 'Yes, God created it. Why? What's so strange about it, didn't you know?'

Carren replied, "Yes, I knew, but... I met an old man in the forest, and he had the most beautiful trees and flowers growing in his garden – I've never seen plants like those."

Yaya's eyes widen, "Carren, remember the stories of the psycho old man of the forest? Couldn't it be him?"

Carren shook her head and briefly explained what she observed about the old man, it was the peacefulness surrounding him and yes - the loneliness. He also had the cutest dog ever, 'Missy'. "Yaya, you would love the dog. She would remind you of your 'Prince'.

The bell rang, and both dispatched to their classes, with the understanding of meeting during the break.

During the break, Carren told Yaya all about Asaph and the story he told her. She knew Yaya was by nature, curious. Nonchalant Yaya replied, "I wanted to meet your old man, but older people know nothing about high-tech. Stories they can tell, but electronics, it's too farfetched.'

Carren explained she wasn't sure if she wanted to go back and also if she would find the path again.

Yaya insisted they should go, as she couldn't believe a stranger living there, without people being aware of him.

Yaya suggested they took Noe, their cousin along. He was at least a boy and was taller than the average boy his size.

Super excited the two decided to wait for Noe and invited him along with them after school. They got hold of him, explained what they were up to, and he was ready for adventure. He was into the latest technology and experiencing something new, was always exciting to him. He already had a curfew on playing games during the week.

The trio completed their chores at home, jumped their bicycles and ride the familiar trail to the forest. All went well till the end of the trail, and they hid their bikes beneath some overlaying trees.

Carren took the lead, and to her surprise, she knew the way. She stopped and showed them the entrance to the place.

Noe was the first to respond, throwing his hands upwards, 'Carren here is nothing else than trees and trees and more trees. Where did you see a cottage? Everyone would know about it.'

He was still busy talking when she pushed him. A gasp left his lips and Yaya looking wide-eyed at Carren as to why she pushed him when next moment she was pushed too.

What they saw were beautiful, as all of a sudden they were in a different world. One would never believe someone lived here. Carren was right. This place was beyond beautiful and somehow magical. The grass had a golden shine to it, and Yaya blinked her eyes to make sure what she saw was real.

Missy came running towards Carren, and the latter picked her up and she was licked all over her face.

Carren boldly walked towards Asaph and introduced her two cousins. Asaph's smile broadened, as happiness filled his heart. He greeted the children with a refreshing glass of homemade juice and Yaya and Noe gave a somewhat insecure smile, not sure how to react.

Carren introduced her cousins to Asaph, and the latter welcomed them. Carren told him they dismissed the idea of him using high-tech equipment that made stories seemed real. She smiled, looked at Asaph and asked to share the story of yesterday. As she was ready to listen to the remainder of the story.

Asaph took his book and started telling them the story of the creation.

'Thousands of years back, the earth was void. There was nothing, only waters and dark. You could see nothing in front of you. Then God decided that he would like to transform the void in seven days.

Noe kicked Carren and whispered, "Where's the high-tech you spoke about."

Asaph overheard Noe and knew the reason for him coming along. He wanted to experience what Carren saw the day before.

Asaph put the book down and took his hands and spread it out, almost as though working on an interactive whiteboard.

Up pop this massive scenery of darkness with a spirit or something hovering over it.

Carren heard the same deep but gentle, loving voice as the day before. "Let there be heaven and earth."

The sound was almost unbearable as everything in front of their eyes started to move.

Shocked filled the children's hearts, as this was a bit different from the day before.

The narrator continued, "Let there be light." The deep dark formless mass disappeared and there was light. It was as though the Creator was an onlooker to the story, or the narrator himself, but this was scary, yet fascinating. "I'll call the light "day," and the darkness "night." The light was intense, and the children had to look away.

"And there was evening, and there was morning – the first day. When the word "evening" was uttered, all became dark, even where they sat, but instantly it became "morning", and it was day again.

The children saw the massive waters, and it seemed as though it would wet them. They moved backwards and heard the voice again, "Let there be a vault between the waters to separate water from water. You'll be "sky". The sky formed. Carren, Yaya and Noe were on the edge of what happened in front of their eyes.

At once, they saw a giant hand moved the water aside, and they could see land. Instantly vegetation sprout at speed and they distinguished all sort of plants. It was almost as though the earth was on the move, and they could see what grew where. They saw Asaph's garden and recognised the trees present here.

The voice continued, "Let the dry ground be "land" and the waters "seas". The end of day three.

Asaph asked the children, "did you know the entire water fits Gods' hand?"

Noe was first to respond, "Oh no, it cannot be! Water slips through ones fingers when scooped. No, I don't think that would be possible. But is it for real? It sounds unbelievable."

Asaph saw the confusion on the children' faces and picked up the old book and opened it. Carren sneaked over and saw on top on the left, was written Isaiah 42.

Asaph started to read, "Who else has held the oceans in his hand? Who has measured off the heavens with his fingers? Who else knows the weight of the earth or has weighed the mountains and hills on a scale?"

Yaya burst with excitement, "It is true, my Sunday school teacher told us the story, but I thought it was just a story." She leaned over and read the scripture. A warm sensation ran through her body as she followed Asaph's old wrinkled finger. A smile covered her face as she quietly uttered. "Wow, but this God is massive!"

They saw a massive pointy finger with a direct order, "sun, moon and stars fill your places, and you'll mark seasons, days and years. Sun, you will give light during the day, and you the lesser one "moon', you will give light at night, along with the stars."

Instantly all appeared in front of their eyes, and the children glued to the seating on the grass. It felt like a 3D movie. Yaya looked at her two cousins and said, "It looks so real. Now I understand how Pa was able to tell us when the wind will blow or it will rain. Remember, in the little fishing town they lived, he always said when the sun rises and shone bright early morning, the wind would blow, and it did."

"Yaya I know, but we can talk later."

The voice and scenery continued, "Let the water be full of living creatures." Instantly all types of sea animals appeared, by the thousand in different shapes and colours.

"Birds, fly above the earth across the vault of the sky." Birds of all sizes and colours instantly started to fly – they just appeared and off they flew in various directions.

"Be blessed, be fruitful and increase in number and fill the water in the seas, and birds, increase on the earth."

After each word uttered, things just happened. The fish started to multiply, the birds increased, and it was the fifth day.

The voice continued and said, "Land, produce living creatures according to their kinds; livestock, the creatures that move along the ground, and the wild animals, each according to its kind." From the land, living creatures started to pop up and instantly ran, each group in their kind.

"I'll create mankind in my image, male and female."

Then they heard the order, "Be fruitful and increase in number; fill the earth and subdue it. Rule over the fish in the sea and the birds in the sky. And over every living creature that moves on the earth."

As the voice spoke, it was almost like a slide show with all the sea, and land animals with humanity given dominium over them.

"To think we received dominium to rule," Noe whispered.

Carren agreed and looked at Asaph and felt as though she would love him, to be her new grandfather. He was so lonely. He had no one to talk to, and she decided there and then, that she would visit him every day. She would bring other children along to listen to his stories, and then he wouldn't be alone. Luckily he had Missy around, but she knew dogs could not take the place of people. We all need one another.

Asaph continued, unaware of Carren's thoughts, 'That dear children, is the story of the creation.'

Noe had a lot of question and wanted to know why God made the snake and scorpion. They were dangerous creatures and are of no good to people. Noe continued and said one of his friends almost died after a snake bit him.

Asaph looked at the children and said, that was a story for another day, as to why snakes bite people. In the Garden of Eden, all lived in harmony, until the snake enticed the woman, called Eve and the peace was disturbed, as God cursed the snake. But that would be a story for another day.

He turned around and walked into his house and brought out some fresh mango juice he made. The children looked at each other when they saw the old fashioned clay cups, but didn't say a word.

Asaph invited them to help themselves, which they did. When they drank the first sip, it had a refreshing sweetness they never knew juice could have and asked him how he made them and where he got the mangos.

He explained the fruit garden was a few meters away and he'll take them on a little tour by next week. You would be spoiled with a different juice daily and perhaps time would allow him to teach them to make their juice.

The three were super excited and after drinking the juice, told Asaph they had to go home before their parents start looking for them. Carren, Yaya and Noe greeted and left through the hedge of trees. They walked, collected their bicycles and drove home.

Before they reached home, they stopped at the nearby park and shared everything Asaph told them. They were excited about sharing. They were unaware of the janitor of their school standing nearby and overheard their talk.

A frown appeared on his face, as he realised that the children were visiting some stranger in the forest. He made up his mind to follow them the next day to make sure he overheard correctly. All the people spoke of the psycho of the forest for years, but no one knew where he lived. Perhaps these children can lead him to the psycho's place, and the police can capture the psycho, and he could become a hero. The janitor gave a big smile and was just on his way to sneak off when Carren turned around and caught him overhearing their conversation.

He grabbed his bag and wanted to walk away when Carren's voice stopped him in his track, 'What are you doing? Why are you eavesdropping our conversation?'

The school janitor, was known for his curiosity. He always informed the parents about what their children do at school. He was such a sly guy and the children wish the school could appoint a new janitor.

He swallowed his breath and denied Carren's accusation, "I didn't eavesdrop. My bag fell and I picked it up." But his face was covered with guilt, and he couldn't wait to get away from the children. He hated it when they put him on the spot.

Yaya was the first one to talk and instructed Carren to let go of him, as he would deny till chickens start to fly. They let go of the janitor but knew they needed to be careful when visiting Asaph, as they didn't want their parents to find out.

Day 2: The 10 Commandments

Children Followed After School

The trio was super excited to visit Asaph that afternoon, and each one told a close friend or two of all the things Asaph shared with them. They gave a little description of the place and the atmosphere and their friends decided they want to join them visiting the old man, as they loved stories.

The entire day the janitor watched the children's every move and knew they would revisit the forest that afternoon. He decided to follow them, and as soon as they jumped their bicycles, he got on his.

The children were unaware of the school janitor following, but one of the girls swerved for a squirrel and almost fell. She came to a halt and inspected her bicycle. All the children stopped, assisted her, and who cycled around the corner? The school janitor.

He tried to hit the brakes of his bicycle, but too late. They spotted him. As one they jumped their bikes again, and Noe screamed, "Speed!" The children speed and before long, the janitor was out of sight.

Breathless, they hid their bikes and made their way to Asaph's house. When Asaph saw more children, his heart was glad. He looked at them and was concerned and a frown visible between his eyes. "What happened, why are all of you out of breath?"

Carren was the first to answer, "Nothing much. We decided to race each other." She knew it was partly the truth but was afraid that the Asaph would not let them revisit him, as they would put his life in danger.

Asaph gave each child an ice-cold berry drink with frost running down the glass. It seemed filled with crush ice, but it was just different. The taste was one the children had never drunk before.

Yaya wanted to know where he got the delicious sweet berries, and he replied when it's time he would introduce them to all his fruit trees. He will take them on tour to see the healthy and big fruit in his garden. He hoped time would allow him to show the children.

The children looked at one another, and a buzzing noise aroused as they tried to figure out all the substances used for the berry drink.

The janitor tried as hard as he could to follow the children, but they were soon out of sight, and it seemed as though instantly they disappeared. He decided to go left from the bicycle trail to see if he could spot the children when his front wheel hit an animal trap.

Upset and frustrated, he kicked the damaged wheel and knew he had to walk the long way home. He started pushing his bicycle in the direction of the town and made his mind. He would catch them all and inform their parents. The psycho should be caught and sent to prison.

The children had forgotten about the janitor, and Carren introduced the new children to Asaph. All felt instantly at home, and Asaph looked up - and gave a smile.

Asaph asked them about the Ten Commandments, and some children acknowledge, they were familiar with them but didn't know them in detail.

Yaya told them she knew about it, as her Sunday school teacher taught them the Ten Commandments. She explained her two favourite one. Honour your father and your mother so that you may live long, and you shall not steal."

Noe's eyes went bigger, as he knew how he disobeyed his parents when they asked him to switch off his games. And all the food he stole from his sister's plate and at times the fridge?

Asaph saw the surprises on the other children' faces and calmed them. Asaph gently offered, "Let me tell you more about the Ten Commandments we should live by." Asaph was on the verge to open his mouth when the clouds became dark. A frown crept between his eyes, and he wondered why the weather suddenly changed.

They all looked up and noticed how the clouds above made a white type of garment – a massive one. It covered the entire air above them. All glued to the grass and no one could move.

Next, they heard a deep voice spoke from the dark cloud, "I'm the Lord your God." There was a long pause. The children and Asaph looked up and followed the voice in the dark clouds, filled with love, but yet firm. "I am the Lord your God, who brought you out of Egypt, out of the land of slavery."

Again the children frowned as to wonder when they were in Africa. Yaya tried to calm the children and said it was thousands of years back, but they were fortunate to hear it from God himself. As from His mouth only comes truth.

The deep, loving voice continued, "You shall have no other gods before me." Again the pause before He continued. "You shall not make yourself an image in the form of anything in heaven above, or on the earth beneath, or in the waters below. Then the pause again, almost as though the words should sink in.

"You shall not bow down to them or worship them; for I, the Lord your God, am a jealous God. I punish the children for the sin of the parents to the third and fourth generation of those who hate me—but showing love to a thousand generations of those who love me and keep my commandments.

The children's' mouths opened and gasped could be heard as they shared amongst one another, "We would get punished for our parents' sin. I don't think our parents' sin. They know what is right from wrong.'

The voice continued, "You shall not misuse the name of the Lord your God, for the Lord will not hold anyone guiltless who misuses his name."

Noe's mouth opened, and he immediately thought of his Physical Education teacher. He would always criticise the children if they couldn't do a specific activity and lashed them with, "My God, get the basics right! Or God, but you are stupid.'

He should get the scripture and warn his PE teacher, not to use the name of God in vain. God doesn't like it. God gently said, "Noe, your thoughts about your teacher is correct. It's a sin to use my name in vain."

Noe thought he would die. God called him by name. Noe suddenly held a more significant admiration for God.

The voice continued, "but you should also, remember the Sabbath day by keeping it holy. Six days you shall labour and do all your work, but the seventh day is a Sabbath to the Lord your God. On it, you shall not do any work, neither you, nor your son or daughter, nor your male or female servant, nor your animals, nor any foreigner residing in your towns."

Smiles appeared on the children's faces when they heard they shouldn't work on a Sunday; for some, they knew it was on a Saturday. That meant no homework on the seventh day!

In six days, the Lord made the heavens and the earth, the sea, and all that is in them, but he rested on the seventh day. Therefore the Lord blessed the Sabbath day and made it holy.

The voice from the dark clouds continued, 'Honour your father and your mother, so that you may live long in the land the Lord your God is giving you."

Stevie was somehow scared when he looked at Asaph and asked, "Will I die young if I disrespect my parents?"

As Asaph opened his mouth to answer, the Lord continued speaking, "You shall not murder. You shall not commit adultery. You shall not steal. You shall not give false testimony against your neighbour. You shall not covet your neighbour's house. You shall not covet your neighbour's wife, or his male or female servant, his ox or donkey, or anything that belongs to your neighbour."

The children now totally overwhelmed with what was just said. Their eyes still focussed on the thick clouds, when it started to clear up and little clouds with the name God began to form and came down. The children simultaneously opened their hands, and the word came resting on their fingers and started to infiltrate their fingers. They felt a light tangible feeling as it moved up their left arm and landed in their hearts.

All the children's right hands simultaneously moved to their heart and sealed their hearts. Carren whispered, "God now lives in our hearts. We have heard him and saw his name coming down and enter our hearts."

Yaya, whispered, "Wise King Solomon mentioned it in his Proverbs."

Asaph explained, "Yes, King Solomon wrote it in his Proverbs, my son, keep my words and store up my commands within you...Keep my commandments, and you will live; guard my teachings as the apple of your eye. Bind them on your fingers; write them on the tablet of your heart."

The children started to ask questions. It was the first time they heard the Ten Commandments, the way God explained it. They wanted to know where they could get hold of it, and Asaph walked over to his big book and opened it in front at Exodus 20 and started to read the verse.

More and more questions came from the children, as their hearts filled with curiosity. They wanted to know what happened to the stones and Asaph told them Moses was assigned to build an Ark for the Lord's commandments. But today, no one knows where it was.

The children were intrigued by all the information, and they have to share the news with their parents, but knew if they did, their parents would want to know who told them. Amy suggested they should ask their Religious and Moral Education teacher to make them copies of the Ten Commandments and give them a quiz as well. They'll take their books home and ask their parents for help.

All agreed it to be a great plan and decided to do just that.

After the children left, Asaph sat at his table with a cup of tea, praising the Lord for what he had done. There was such a presence of the Lord present this afternoon. His heart was in a happy state, as he full-filled what was expected of him, to tell the next generation of the marvellous things the Lord had done.

He hoped the children would pitch till the end. He knew if the others decided to stay, Carren would come daily. She had a heart filled with love. Carren was such a loving child, and so Noe and Yaya. He hoped their parents embraced the love of their children.

A smiled covered his face, as the best thing ever happened to him lately, was Carren falling through the hedge and landed on his premises. He longed going home. He couldn't wait to share everything he had to share, for these children to one day tell their children about the praiseworthy deeds of the Lord.

If every child knows the truth, they would put their trust only in God and no one else. Not the clothes, neither shoes that they wear, but God. Then they would never forget God's marvellous deeds and would keep all his commandments.

He enjoyed God's commandments all over again and was pleased for the way God revealed Himself to the children. God, filled with love as His nature is love, but most people want to see him as an angry God. He knew the children would portray the love they'd experienced God.

When the children knew the works of the Lord and everything he would share with them, they would not be such a stubborn and rebellious generation like their ancestors. Their ancestors had seen so much of the power and wonders of God, but their hearts were not loyal to God, and he knew it. Their spirits were not faithful to him.

God made our hearts, so he knows everything within it, as it is always said, "Out of the heart will only flow what was in there." Asaph decided to call it a day, as he felt exhausted and went in. Tomorrow is another day.

Day 3: Plagues

School Janitor Attacked By Bees

Their friends dispatched, each to their respective homes and Carren invited her cousins to a drink at her house. The three sat at the kitchen table and discussed all the happenings, and were excited to know more.

Carren took them up to the attic and said it would be more private to talk there. She told her mom they would be in the attic. Her mom replied it was a bit dusty, but they should clean a bit and chill.

The three ran the stairs, and Carren flung the attic door open and all were searching, but didn't know what? Perhaps they were looking for a book like Asaph. They wanted to read by themselves what was in there.

It was Noe, that got hold of a similar book, and when he picked it up, an old round bronze coin rolled from it. It spun and fell on its face. Written on it, 'the plagues of Egypt and other.' They could see it was an ancient outdated coin and wondered why it was locked in the book.

They opened the book and saw a space where it slotted with an inscription.

Please put back, never twist the coin. Yaya ordered Noe to slot it into its place, but Noe, as his cousins knew him, wanted to know why. "Why shouldn't I twist it?" She tried to grab it, but he jumped away and sat opposite the two of them with the coin and a broad smile to his face. The girls shrugged their shoulders and decided to ignore him. They then convinced him to take it to Asaph and asked him what it meant. Noe put the coin back into its slot and closed the book.

He uttered irritably through his breath, "stupid girls. Always wants to do things by the book."

The next day, the children planned their trip at school, and Carren told the rest they got a similar book with a coin locked inside. They'll take the book along to Asaph that afternoon, perhaps he could inform them about the inscription on the coin, and why spinning was forbidden.

The janitor watched the children and tried to follow two of the other children. He overheard what they said and gave a satisfying smile. He knew they were up to mischief. Today, he will leave earlier and wait under an overhang in the forest and follow them from there.

After school, all the children as planned headed for the forest and couldn't wait to get to Asaph. On their way, they saw a commotion in front of them, and a guy carried on a stretcher. All the children neared and what they saw shocked them. On it lie their school janitor, with a swollen face. They overheard the people saying, 'bee-stung'. The children looked at each other, and the school janitor saw them and wanted to say something, but his lips way too swollen to utter a word. The people asked him to be calm; they'll get him to a hospital soon.

The children continued their ride and felt sorry for the janitor, but what made him come out here alone? They should be careful, as he was up to something. He knew they were visiting someone, but he didn't have proof. They knew him. He forever informed their parents what they were doing at school, and when they get home, they would be put to house arrest or given chores as punishment.

The children hid their bikes and by foot walked to Asaph's place. Missy welcomed them as usual, and the most refreshing strawberry drinks awaited their arrival. Asaph was dear to them, and Carren wondered what she could give him to say thank you. It was as though he read her mind and smiled. "Bringing your friends along to listen to my stories is the greatest gift you could have given me. You will find out real soon why."

Carren excitedly gave him the book and explained where she found it. Asaph opened the book and took a deep breath as his eyes popped with surprise and sparkled with excitement.

There was excitement in his voice when he asked, "Where did you get hold of this book?"

"In our attic, I think it might belong to my late grandpa."

Noe jumped up and told Asaph he should look at the coin in the book. It had an inscription and an instruction. And why they shouldn't spin the coin.

Asaph looked at the children through pierced eyes and said, "The coin when turned bring things to life. It will cause a simulation, and you would experience everything that happened centuries back, as though it was today."

Noe excitedly asked the others if they would also like to see for real what had happened. All the children agreed, and it seemed as though they had no fear. Before Asaph could speak another word, Noe had taken the coin and spun it.

The children's sat breathless, as they saw a massive simulation of what looked like two people captured in an argument. On the one figure that looked like an

Egyptian god, stood the word, "Pharaoh" and on the other character, "Moses".

The children' eyes locked on the figure Moses and behind him was as though a story trail took place.

The children saw how soldiers visited a village and took young boys and babies from their parents. They looked ruthless, with hateful eyes.

They opened the baby's pants and some were taken and others left. Then children soon realised the soldiers left the girl babies and took the boy babies. Mothers grieving cries echoed the entire village. The latter sadden the children.

The children' eyes fixed on a household, and they could see the anxiety on the mother's face, as she put down a black pot and inspected what looked like a basket. She wrapped a baby in blankets, put it in the basket and gave it to a young girl their age. She opened the door and looked left and right, almost as to see if everything was safe.

At the distance, the children saw those soldiers taking the boy babies were marching on their way to the house with the baby in the basket.

The children held their breath as they knew the young girl had to escape with the baby. "Hurry, they whispered, run!" The girl slipped out and when she came around the corner of her house, started to run. Meantime her mother packed away everything inside, so there was no trace of a baby. She inspected the room for the last time and hoped she didn't miss a thing.

The soldiers banged on her door and pushed it open. The lady bumped aside, and the place inspected. They looked one last time at the mother and left. Relieved, she fell on her knees, covered her face as tears ran down her cheeks. She looked up, and they could see she whispered, almost like praying.

Then they saw the twelve-year-old girl with the basket, running to what looked like the river. Halfway, she was breathless and put the basket down. She looked over her shoulder and saw the soldiers at a distance and started to run again. Sweat formed on her face, and one could see the basket became too heavy for the girl.

Carren and all the children started to sheer the girl. "Run, you can make it. Go, go. They are on your trail" – as though the girl could hear them.

What seemed like ages, the girl reached the waters and looked one last time at the smiling baby and let go.

The children saw the eyes of a crocodile above the water, and it swam towards the basket.

Some children closed their eyes, unwilling to witness the scene about to play off in front of their eyes.

As the crocodile opened its mouth, its eyes widened. The children saw an outline of a massive right hand pressing hard on the mouth of the crocodile. Its tail curled and it looked as though it was in pain. The hand released its mouth, and the crocodile quickly turned around and swam in the opposite direction. The other crocodiles started to swim towards the basket and followed it downstream.

Meanwhile, the girl was tired. She kept on running along the river shore with her eyes fixed on the basket. Now and then she looked ahead of her and stumbled over a stone on her path. She grabbed her big toe, saw the blood, but kept her momentum and ran. She knew it was a matter of life and death, and she couldn't take her eyes off the basket.

She ran, but the children could sense she was tired. They felt pity for her but cheered her to keep running. She stopped trying to get her breath back, and the basket drifted ahead of her. The basket took a sudden turn - out of sight.

Her eyes widened as fear covered her face, and she started to run again.

The children were tense, and uttered small pleas, "Please, please let the baby be safe, oh God give her more strength to follow the basket." It was Yaya sending up a small little prayer.

The girls' face struck and eyes wide as she came around the bend and eyes searching the waters for a trail of the basket. A sadness covered her face, as she realised she lost it, but then from the tall grass, she saw a movement, and the next moment it was visible and moved downstream again. This time she didn't take her eyes from the basket and just ran along.

The children applaud, and laughter arose in Asaph's garden when they saw the basket with the baby again.

A beautiful lady busy bathing in the river, saw the basket drifting her way. She stretched her hand and took the basket and looked into it. The baby gave the cutest smile, and she smiled back. She picked the baby from the basket and held him against her chest.

The girl waited for her breath to return. Washed her face and approached the lady, "You have a beautiful baby. Are you perhaps looking for a babysitter? I know someone who is great with babies."

The lady holding the baby looked at the young girl and said, "Yes, I'm looking for one. Do you know someone?

The young girl nodded and replied she would fetch her. She turned around and ran back to fetch Moses' mom, who became his babysitter.

The next scene was fast forward. The children saw the young child running around a palace. Then sitting in the library to read, until he was a grown man, the one they saw standing in front of the Pharaoh and was in a heated discussion with him.

And so the story of Moses in Egypt before Pharaoh unfold. The words, "Let my people go!" trailed and entered each child's ear. It was almost as though they sat on the edge of their seat, looking at what happened.

The two out of ancient times, with old fashioned clothing, spoke to one another. One could sense there was tension between the two as the one spoke, "My Lord said, you should let His people go."

The other one looking like an Egyptian god, retaliated with the words, "Moses, who are your people. I am Pharaoh, king of Egypt. Who are you to instruct me in my palace as what to do? I'm king. I raised you in my palace. My daughter gave you the best education, but you decided to become the spokesperson for the Israelites. And, no, I cannot let them go!"

The children saw the frown on Moses's and his brother's Aaron's face, and the next moment Aaron lifted his staff. They held their breath as – it seemed he wanted to hit Pharaoh, but then he threw his staff on the floor, and it changed into a big snake.

It seemed as though the act didn't move Pharaoh, and he called his wise men and sorcerers and asked them to throw down their staffs and show Moses what theirs could do.

Prideful they stepped near and threw their staffs. To the children's surprise, they were small snakes, and Aaron's snake started to move forward and swallowed the first one. The snakes came from all directions to attack his one, but one after the other, it swallowed the little ones until there was none.

The children clapped hands and Noe said, "Don't play with Moses and Aaron, they will free their people. Moses is not afraid of you, Pharaoh." The children asked Noe to be quiet as they wanted to see what happened next.

Pharaoh was white with anger when he saw what happened and started to scream on his sorcerers and magicians. "Out! You useless men, out!" They couldn't wait to get out of Pharaoh's sight, as his hand was on a sword attached to his left.

"Moses, look out for the sword", some girls shouted."

Aaron stretched his hand, and the snake changed into his staff again. And the next moment it was in his hand.

The children sitting on the ground applaud the scenery they had just witnessed.

The scenery were shifted to the Nile River and the children were all ears and eyes, awaiting what would happen next. Moses had walked up to Pharaoh and asked him to let God's people go, but Pharaoh didn't answer him and stared over the Nile, full of himself, as though he created the Nile. Then Moses lifted his hand and struck the water.

Pharaohs eyes widened, and a hardness covered his mouth, as he looked at the bloody water. The water turned into blood and instantly, fish came to the surface and drifted – all dead. Aaron also lifted his sword, and they could hear the guards screaming from the palace, "blood, and blood everywhere."

The children observed the ladies busy with laundry at the river, and as the water turned into blood, their entire washing covered in blood. They threw the washing garments down and screamed. All started to run, as they didn't know what happened.

Pharaoh turned around and hurried to his palace. A grin to his face and hard lines around his mouth. The children heard between his breaths, "I won't let them go!"

Moses looked at Pharaoh and said, "The Lord my God said you should let His people go to worship Him, but you are stubborn, He will hit the Nile, your palace and everything with a plague of frogs."

Pharaoh gave a smirked and dismissed Moses's words.

Moses looked at Aaron, his brother, whom God had given to his assistance and nodded his head. "It was time to act out what the Lord had said." They saw Aaron looking at the waters of Egypt. He lifted his hand and stretched it over the waters of Egypt and frogs came up in the thousands, uncountable.

The children gasped for breath, as they saw how the frogs started to hop in every direction. Within minutes the entire palace was covered with frogs, the streets, people's houses, their pots – frogs were everywhere.

The children put their hands over their ears as the sound the frogs made was to drive any sane person crazy.

Moses and Aaron walked casually, and where they stepped, the path was clean, but people screamed, and it was chaos.

The simulation ended, and the children were in awe of what they have seen. A deep hunger for more arose within them, and they couldn't believe all this happened. They didn't know the content of the black book, was this thrilling?

They all bombarded Asaph with questions and a smile crept to his face as he took the thick book and page to the scripture and started reading it. The children looked at Asaph and said he was the best storyteller and one by one, the children jumped up and hugged him.

He went in and brought a fresh juice, this time an orange juice, but the best they had ever had. While drinking and excitedly talking, he told them it was time to go home, before their parents got worried.

The children reasoned their parents should also be present and experience what they do. Still, Carren told them it would not be wise, as they had all contradict the first rule of safety, 'Don't talk to strangers.' And Asaph was a stranger to their parents. The children agreed, and their faces glowed, with the excitement of what they had seen.

Noe was the first one to jump up and took the coin, slot it back into the book and put it in his backpack, ready to ride home. It seemed as though the children didn't want to leave the peacefulness of the garden, but Yaya told them they had to go. They can come back tomorrow again.

The children wanted to know if they can watch the rest of the plagues the next day. Asaph told them, depending if Noe brought the book along and spun the coin, then they will be able to see the simulation again.

Noe promised he would bring it along, but they just want to put it back in the attic in case Carren's mom would search the book. Not that they think she would.

The children greeted Asaph and left. The latter had a smile to his face, looked up and thanked the Lord. His spirit was filled with excitement, as he was going home within due time. Eventually, he would be able to walk the streets made of gold. It was a long wait. He thought he would never leave. He sat, staring in front of him and thought he had to prepare the children, especially Carren.

Day 4: The Plagues Continue

Hospital Janitor Spy On The Children

They reached home, and Noe gave the book to Carren to replace in the attic should her mother or father look for it.

Carren ran the stairs book in her hand. Her mother called her name and was at the bottom of the stairs. She wanted to know where she was off every afternoon as she was seldom home. Carren tried to hide the big black book, but her mom's eyes didn't miss a thing.

"What is that in your hand Carren?" her mom asked.

Carren looked around as though stunned with her mother's question and thought of something to say.

The next moment she put on a sad face and when

she spoke there was a longing in her voice, "I missed

Pa, so I took the big book he sometimes had next to his bedside and held it close to me. It still has his smell, you know." Carren hoped her mom would bite what she had just said.

To her surprise, her mom came walking up the stairs, made her sit and held her. She spoke with a gentle voice, "Carren, I also miss my dad at times, but he is at a better place. If it would make you feel better, you can keep the book at your bedside, and you may have it if it means so much to you."

Tears started to run freely, both for the longing of her Pa and for her receiving one of his most precious possession.

Her mom let her go and said when she was ready, she should come help laying the table for supper. Carren nodded and ran up the attic to be alone with her thoughts. She looked at the book and realised it was hers now. She paged through it and saw it had an old testament and a new testament. She scanned the Old Testament and saw the name Lord and God appeared all the time, but in the New Testament, the name Jesus appeared most of the time. She should not forget to ask Asaph about the two books.

She took her phone and texted Noe and Yaya about the book her mother gave her. They were super excited, and all agreed to meet again after school and headed the now familiar road to the forest.

Next day at school all was normal, except for the janitor being around. News spread fast about him being in hospital due to bee-stung. He would be out soon, as the antibiotics worked against the stung.

The children looked at one another and knew they shouldn't feel glad, but they were happy that he was not around. He always eavesdropped their conversations, and they don't want anyone to know about their visits to the forest. The stories were exciting, and they wanted to hear them all!

At the hospital, the janitor laid in pain and a friend of him; the hospital janitor was visiting him. It wasn't long before he told his friend about the children seeing someone in the forest. He insisted it to be the psycho old man, but he wasn't sure. He asked his friend to follow the children the next day, as they had to pass the hospital. His friend agreed and would report what he saw. The hospital janitor couldn't wait to follow the children the next day.

He planned to go ahead of them to the forest and wait there. This week he only worked till one o'clock, so he would have sufficient time to wait and hide at the entrance of the forest – the way of the walking trail.

The next day the children hasted to the forest. Noe dropped the heavy book in his backpack, and all met at the entrance of the trail. They were unaware of the hospital janitor watching them. He saw them hiding their bicycles. He instantly knew his friend was right; these children visited someone, but who?

He saw them looking around for any trace of being followed, and when they saw no one around, they walked off in a hurry. He knew he would find the truth today and should it be the psycho they thought it was, the children would be in great danger. He shook his head and didn't want to think about it.

The hospital janitor followed them and saw how one by one, they pushed aside some overhanging trees and disappeared behind it. When the last child climbed through, he waited a few minutes, not sure what to expect behind the hedge, as one would never believe some activity was taking place, but the children disappeared in there.

He went nearer and moved the hedge and close it again. It was real, behind it was the most beautiful place, such green grass and beautiful garden he had never seen. He was too afraid to look again, as it seemed mystical and he was too scared to be spotted. He wanted to turn around and mark the place, but then he heard some commotion inside and tried to peep what it was.

He peeped and saw this massive simulation of Egypt. He knew it was Egypt because of the pyramids. The children, unaware of being watched excitedly, continued watching the simulation.

They saw a figure written Aaron, and he stretched his staff. The children immediately tensed as they knew something was about to happen. The next moment the dust turned into lice and the people started to scratch. It was everywhere, even on their animals. Pharaoh's palace swarm of lice, and a hardness appeared on his face.

Noe spoke and pointed to the simulation, "Let God's people go, and can't you see how your people and animals are suffering?"

Yaya asked him to calm down, as they don't want to attract attention. This garden and book were magical; they might be drawn into the story.

The janitor's mouth fell open. It seemed so real. Before he could think about it all, another scenery took place and this time the children, and he dug. The simulation moved over their heads, and it was just swarms of flies everywhere. They laid eggs, and one could see the small whitish worms everywhere. It was a mess.

The gasp of the janitor made all faces turn to the left of the hedge where they came through. They knew someone was watching and immediately knew there was trouble.

Noe jumped up and opened the hedge and saw the shocking face of the hospital janitor. Before he could say a thing, Asaph invited him in to join the children, as he would explain everything to him. The warmth and friendliness of Asaph draw the hospital janitor from his hiding place and he joined the children. An excitement present on his face.

They saw the mess and destruction the flies caused in Egypt. Moses and Aaron, along with all the Israelites, had no flies. Their camp was clean.

The children were amazed as to how it could be. The places so near to one another, but the Egyptians bombarded with flies.

Then they saw Moses and Pharaoh in conversation, and it seemed as though they banged heads. So they heard Pharaoh's words reaching their ears, "I will let you go, that you may sacrifice to the Lord your God in the wilderness; only you shall not go very far away. Intercede for me." Moses nodded and prayed to the Lord. They saw a large hand, and their hearts started to beat faster, as they knew it was the hand of the Lord. The children were in awe and unbelief as the hand swept away the flies.

They looked at one another and shook their heads, asking if they saw what just happened. With big eyes, the boys said God was their new superhero.

Even the janitor was as excited at the children. He was fascinated and wanted to see more.

They saw the hardness on Pharaohs face again and Yaya sighed, "Why doesn't he want to listen? Can't he see how his people suffer every time a new plague hits them? Look, look – I think that is his advisors talking to him. He's so adamant, he just dismissed them and chased them off with his hand." The children agreed, and all wondered when he would learn?

The children saw thick clouds appeared and a rumbling noise as turbulent whether hit Egypt and the palace of Pharaoh again. A massive dark shape of a hand was over Egypt, and one after the other they saw life stock fell. They saw cattle, horses, donkeys, camels and other animals fell dead, even the sheep.

People stood at their livestock and farmers started to cry as their entire savings were just lost. Families started moaning and pointed to the Israelites camp and said someone just brought news. Their livestock was as healthy and alive as could be.

Pharaoh promised Moses he will let his people go and the plague stopped.

The children saw Pharaoh standing at the river early morning, and Moses alongside him. Both were speechless, but Pharaoh had a frown on his forehead, and his face was hard. It looked as though he wanted to take his sword and attack Moses and Aaron, but both lifted their hands and threw the ashes they took from a Furness up to heaven.

Boils broke out in sores on man and beast. The people cried of pain.

The girls started to cry along and begged Pharaoh to let the people of the Lord go. "Can't he see the pain your people are in?" There were cries all over Egypt and parents tried to nurture their children with plants, but it seemed helpless.

Again Pharaoh promised to let the people go and wanted to see Moses.

Carren gave one look at Pharaohs" face and said, "Guys, he won't listen. Look at his face. It has the same hard look to it as all the other times when he said he would let them go and didn't. What's wrong with the guy?"

Before the children could continue their conversation, they saw Moses and Pharaoh again in conversation and heard Moses' words. His tone was serious when he spoke, "The Lord said you should let His children go, or He will send hail on the land none that Egypt ever had. Get your livestock and all your people from the fields."

Pharaoh looked at Moses and with his hand, brushed it away. Some palace officials had smirks on their faces, but others started to run from there, warning their relatives and friends.

Moms turned to idols, praying for the safety of their children and husbands. They knew how hard the plagues hit them, but not the Israelites. Pharaoh should just let them go.

Next moment Moses lifted his staff towards heaven and an unbearable noise filled the sky. The children blocked their ears as they saw. Hail started to fall. It appeared as though it fell on them; it felt real! Fire mingled with hail. It was cumbersome, and people fearfully whispered, "There was never hail like this in the land of Egypt as long as we lived."

They saw every part of Egypt struck with hail on all that was in the field. Some man that didn't adhere to the message started running looking for shelter, but it was too late. Man and beast, all the herbs of the field and trees began to broke and fell. It was chaos, as the animals didn't know where to run.

Yaya shouted, "Let it stop, please let it stop. I can't look anymore."

Asaph quickly took the coin and placed it in the book sitting next to Noe. Everything became quiet, and the children were partly traumatised. Asaph didn't know what to do, as he realised it was too heavy for them to watch, as the shock was visible on the faces. He looked up, and a few words left his lips.

A gentle breeze of peace filled the entire garden. Within seconds laughter was all around the garden, and they discussed all the happenings in Egypt and wanted to know when Pharaoh will let the people go. The hospital janitor replied, Pharaoh being a very hard-headed king. He thought he was the mightiest ruler in the world, but he was human and God was the Creator of all heaven and earth. The Lord made us all, and he knew each of us by name.

The children looked as Asaph and wanted to know if it was true, will God be able to remember all the names of people in every country. Also the confusing names to pronounce? Asaph nodded his head, "remember, God is God; there is none like him." He took the book from Noe and page to a specific page and read from it. "Children in Jeremiah 1:5 it reads, "Before I formed you in the womb I knew you, before you were born I set you apart..."

Noe was surprised that after all these years the Lord knew him. So he formed me in my mother's womb. Noe shook his head in disbelief to this great God of theirs. He never knew He was that great!

Yaya looked at Asaph and stated, "There were more plagues, see that you have the book in your hand, do you want to tell us what happened next?" All the children agreed, as the simulation was a bit too real.

Asaph sent a basket of fruit around, for the children to eat. The basket filled with the best red apples, juicy pears, peaches and grapes. With the first bite, juice came running down the cheeks, and they were surprised, as they had never eaten such healthy and juicy fruit.

Being here was so peaceful and magical. Everything the children eat or drank had a taste to it they never experienced. They should ask him what manure he used for his flowers, vegetable and fruit garden. It must be a special fertilizer.

Asaph looked at the children's happy faces, with janitor along with them, all waiting for him to start. He told them the eighth plague were locusts. Locust was everywhere in the houses, the field and it stripped every green leave left, after the hail in Egypt.

The children wanted to know why he was so hard-headed. Asaph replied, Pharaoh thought himself as a god and wanted to be higher than the Lord. Pharaoh thought his riches and rulership over Egypt made him untouchable. Still, he never reckoned with the Creator of all heaven and earth and everything on it.

One of the children asked, "Did he ever listened to the Lord? And if yes, what made him listen?"

Asaph smiled and said, it was deep and painful to all in Egypt. After the locust, darkness hit Egypt. It was so dark; people couldn't see a thing in front of them. Then Pharaoh called Moses again like all the other times before to pray to his God, as he would send the people to worship their Lord, just to be hard-headed and stubborn again. Asaph sighs and said Pharaoh finally listened when all the firstborn died.

The children gasped, "What do you mean, all the firstborns' died." Asaph replied with a serious face, but gentle voice, "It was midnight when the Lord struck down all the firstborn in Egypt. From the firstborn of Pharaoh, who sat on the throne, to the firstborn of the prisoner, and those in dungeons. The Lord even struck all the firstborn of their livestock. The people cried and wept for their losses. Families tried comforting each other, but all were hurt. Only then Pharaoh realised who he was opposing the entire time. It was the Lord of all the earth. The great I Am, that asked, "Is anything too hard for Me" – and the answer - nothing!

During those hours of the night, Pharaoh summoned Moses and Aaron and told them to pack and get up and out. They should leave the Egyptians alone, but before leaving, they should bless him.

The Israelites went to Egyptian homes, and the latter gave articles of silver, gold and clothing. The Lord gave his children favour by the Egyptians, and every Egyptian household unpacked and gave. They just wanted them to leave so that they could be safe.

It was Noe who said he wants to see a simulation of the gifts they got. Before anyone could say a thing, he spun the coin, and the massive simulation appeared. They saw the Israelites walked by the Egyptians men and woman, even children stood ready and gave gifts. When an Egyptian family gave a gift to an Israelite, they fell before their gods, and the Israelites could hear the Egyptians whisper, "Let the gift be enough for the rest of us to live."

When the Israelites left the town of the Egyptians, they had a lot of gifts. They walked with cattle and bags of silver and gold. There was happiness amongst them and smiles covered their faces. Eventually, they could leave Egypt and worshipped their God; they were free!

The people started leaving, family by family and all were excited as they knew the Lord had shown Pharaoh, who was the true God. The Lord was Lord.

He showed his majestic work to Pharaoh and his entire office. Eventually, the latter surrendered, and the Lord's people were free.

The smiles on the Israelites faces were priceless as they started to pack and was on their way to their promised land.

The children heard the songs of worship and praise coming from the Israelites lips, and the children began to sing along. They fell in rhythm, and it was as though they were walking and accompany them. The children along with the hospital janitor sang, and it was as though an angelic choir was present in Asaph's' garden.

Asaph smiled and looked up, thanking his Master for what was happening there. For so many years, decades and centuries he was alone and thought he would never go home, but he knew his time was near. He looked at Carren, and her eyes filled with love. He wondered if he should tell her, but he knew she would not let him go. He sighed and knew the Lord would work out everything for good, for those who trust in him.

The songs stopped, and the children turned back to reality, and their faces glowed. Their spirits ignited in the presence of the Lord. Asaph reminded them, it was time to leave. He didn't want their parents to ask too many questions for their late coming.

The children long-faced packed their goodies for the road home.

Carren turned to the hospital janitor and opened her mouth to ask him to keep their secret. But before she could talk, he smiled and told the children; he would never reveal their secret. He loved what he saw and would like to come along with them daily, as he worked only till one in the afternoon. He would daily wait at the forest entrance. The children looked at one another and let him in. He seemed trustworthy to them.

All greeted and took the path through their secret entrance and head home!

Day 5: The Exodus

Children Captured in the Exodus

The school janitor couldn't wait for his friends' visit, as he wanted to know if he succeeded in following the children. He felt way better. The sharp burning pain of the bee-stung disappeared and only a few red, slightly swollen spots were present. He needed to get out. He'll ask the doctor to dismiss him today. The two of them could plan a way to trap the children.

The hospital janitor decided to be quiet about the children. He popped in and casually spoke, but didn't say a word, but couldn't look at his friend. The school janitor's eyes pierced through his friend, and a disappointment was present on his face when he lashed, "You know where the children were, but you don't want to tell. I know you. When you hide something, you cannot look at my face. I trusted you. I will get out and do it myself, but I will find out."

The hospital janitor wanted to explain, but his friend turned his back and asked him to leave, as he wanted some rest.

He opened his mouth and closed it again. Shrugged his shoulder and knew it was the end of their friendship.

He learned and saw so much. He wanted more. The stories were real. He wanted all the people in town to visit Asaph and listen to the stories, but he knew they would turn against him. He couldn't wait for the next day, to listen to what Asaph would share with them. An excitement overwhelmed him as he was super excited for the next day.

The next day at school, the children gathered during break and excitement and buzz were present as they repeated all that had taken place. They spoke about the hard-headed Pharaoh and his leaders and couldn't believe they were so stubborn. It cost them so much in the end.

Yaya excitedly replied, "To think they gave the Israelites gifts to leave them alone. They were scared of God's people. And remember, they were slaves. Can a master be afraid of a slave!"

All the children jumped in sharing, and happy laughter filled their gathering space. Other children came near as to listen to what they had to say, and they told them story after story. The others wanted to know where they got the news. The children just said in Carren's Grand Pa's book that now belongs to her.

The children wanted to know if they could meet on a Saturday afternoon in the park for Carren to bring the book along and tell them the stories. She agreed, and all were happy, except Carren.

What would her peers think of her with the big book under her arm? Would she be able to tell them the way Asaph did? She needed to speak to Noe and Yaya to help her. They were there from the beginning.

She looked at Noe and Yaya and nervously requested, "Will you help me?"

Noe started to laugh at Carren's face. Why all of a sudden so afraid? "You were so excited to tell us. Now do the same for them."

Carren replied, "It's not the same. I grew up with you, and you are family. They are not even my real friends."

Yaya stepped forward and in her calm voice, asked, "What would Asaph have you done with what he shared with us?"

Carren looked down and answered, "Share the information with others."

Yaya, "Then do it. We will be there to support you, and we can all share what we know. But we won't use the coin at any stage with them. Noe will carry and keep the book, while all of us can share what we know.

They all agreed, and a smile covered Carren's face. The bell rang, and all hasted to their respectful lines.

After school, all jumped their bicycles, and as to meet each other at the set time in the forest. Carren's heart filled with excitement at the thought of the story of the Israelites leaving Egypt. That would be the story Asaph would tell them today. She wondered if the hospital janitor would join them today, as he promised he would.

The school janitor knew people were unaware of his discharge from hospital. He would sneak off to the forest and wait for the children and follow them from a distance. And he did just that.

One by one the children past him, until the last one cycled past, he came from his hiding spot and followed them. The children unaware of being watched continued their ride until at their place of hiding the bicycles. Then they continued walking.

The school janitor became excited, as he knew they were up to something. A big smile broadened his face. Next, he jumped as he felt a hand on his shoulder. He looked up disturbed, just to saw his friend, the hospital janitor put his arm around his shoulder and spoke very loud. He took him and led him in the direction of a bench a few steps back and started to talk loud enough for the children to hear.

The children became aware of the company and froze, but were relieved when they saw their friend directed the school janitor in the opposite direction. He started to talk about everything and what. They knew he was busy distracting him, for them to do what they usually do.

Carren, Noe and Yaya along with the other children, sighed of relieve. They should be careful next time.

Asaph, as usual, were unaware of all the commotion and was grateful to see them again. He gave them a cold drink, and it was the most refreshing drink ever. Noe opened the book and took the coin out. All eyes were on Noe as he was about to spin the coin. Noe looked at the coin and decided to turn it in the opposite direction.

Asaph saw what Noe was about to do, and took a big leap as to stop him, but it was too late.

Next, they felt as though they were flying through the air, became part of the exodus with Moses and the

Israelites. The children's eyes were big when they realised where they were.

Asaph looked at the scenery in front of him and was just as surprised as the children. He immediately saw they were near breakpoint and calmed them. He told them they would be out of here in no time, but he didn't know-how. They were with this group of people. He told them just to follow the group and walk along.

The Israelites were so excited to leave, be free and make sacrifices to their God, that they didn't pay much attention to the group that joined them. Here and there were a frown and strange facial expression of people looking at them, but that was it. The children tagged one another and were surprised at the clothing of the people. They looked strange.

Carren brought the children together as they started blaming Noe. The latter wanted to explain. He didn't know what would happen. He just turned it the other way. Carren told the children there was no time for blame, as they should find a way to stay alive.

They followed the path of all the strange people and anxiety wanted to grip their hearts, as fear arose. Would they ever get out of this time zone they were in?

Suddenly they heard Moses spoke and told all should turn around and camp near the sea for the night, before going ahead.

All the people stopped, and they followed the instructions, while still talking and singing. Neighbours showed one another what they received from the Egyptian people, and all were happy. They were free to worship their God.

Suddenly Carren got a vision and saw the face of Pharaoh. She gasped, and shock was visible on her face. Yaya laid her hand on Carren and wanted to know what was wrong. Carren was speechless with wide eyes and Asaph came near and in his gentle voice tried to comfort her. Still, Carren shook her head, and this time they saw the disbelief on her face when she spoke.

"I had a vision or a glimpse of Pharaoh. He had that same hardened expression on his face when he didn't want the people to go. He is coming for us! And look in front of us is a sea, we will never pass here, we will never see our parents." She gripped Noe by the arm and was about to lash when Yaya reprimanded them it wasn't a time to fight. The other children looked up to them and if they start to lose their cool, the others would as well. She knew and prayed they would see home again, how she didn't know.

Yaya asked Asaph what their chances were of getting home and he answered with a straight face, "Only if someone finds and replace the coin into its original slot."

Yaya gasped and knew they would be locked in this situation, as no one knew about Asaph's place in the forest. Tears started to form in her eyes as she turned around and followed the rest of the Israelites.

They were camping near the water when they saw a patch of dust becoming larger. All eyes watched to see what it was and then they realised it was Pharaoh and his army, a massive one. They drove the chariots like wild people and the calmness and happiness present, change to instant chaos as people jumped up and said they should move. The people were terrified and cried out to the Lord.

They blamed Moses, "Was it because there were no graves in Egypt that you brought us to the desert to die? What have you done to us by bringing us out of Egypt? Didn't we say to you in Egypt, 'Leave us alone; let us serve the Egyptians'? It would have been better for us to serve the Egyptians than to die in the desert!"

People accused him from every direction. He held his hand in the air and answered them, "Do not be afraid. Stand firm and you will see the deliverance the Lord will bring you today. The Egyptians you see today you will never see again. The Lord will fight for you; you need only to be still."

Moses looked at the dust further down and looked at the sky and proclaimed it would be dark any time. Rest, and the Lord will fulfil his promise.

Noe wanted to know if God would dwell amongst them to fight, and he pointed to the massive army coming their way. How would He be able to win them over? Asaph smiled at Noe and assured him the God that he knew, created everything, so nothing was too hard for him.

Then Noe remembered the story of the creation and his heart became at peace. He would like to see the Lord as a warrior.

Carren and the rest of the children calmed after Moses' words, and for the first time, Carren saw a cloud moving over their heads to the back. She wondered what it was, but a peace surpassing all understanding came down on the camp. It lingered behind them and enlightened the area where they were, but as she peeped back, trying to look behind the cloud, she saw it was pitch dark.

Moses told the people not to worry, as it was pitch dark behind the cloud, so it made it impossible for them to move towards them. The Lord helped them until here. He would lead them to safety.

Moses raised his staff and stretched out his hand over the sea. The children' eyes were focussed on him as they didn't know what to expect. As every time Moses lifted his staff, they knew something terrible was about to happen.

Yaya gave a smile, as she knew how this story went but was still not sure what to expect. She was in disbelieve about their exodus with the Israelites.

She wondered why the panic? She experienced the greatness of the Lord in Egypt when God sent out all those plagues, and they were saved. It's just unbelievable how soon these people forgot what the Lord had done, not even years back, but yesterday.

She shook her head but knew all of them one time or the other also doubted if things would ever change and she now realises in those times; she doubted her God. Tears formed in her eyes as she whispered, "Sorry, my Lord, I know today that you are more than able." Yaya quickly whipped her tears as she didn't want the others to notice or create panic again.

To think the Lord was with them all the time. When she saw the cloud a few minutes back, she felt that was sign enough for these people to know who went ahead of them and who followed behind them. He was their cloud by day and fire by night.

Carren hugged Yaya and wanted to know whether she was okay. She nodded. Carren in a gentle voice, "Yaya, I'm so sorry I dragged all of you into this. I should have never told you, Noe and the rest. What if we never see our families again?" Carren's voice started to tremble, but Yaya took hold of both her hands. What I know now, was worth knowing. The experiences and stories were fantastic, and I just know we will get home. How I don't know, but we all will get out of here. Let's stay calm and put our trust in the Lord."

Carren's face lit up as she thanked Yaya for staying so calm the entire time. She admired Yaya's faith, and it immediately stirred hers too.

Exhausted from the days' activities, all of them took refuge next to Asaph, as though he was their father. The last they witnessed was a robust eastern wind blowing over the sea, but they didn't know really why. They all closed their eyes and fell asleep.

A smile covered Asaph's lips as he saw the peacefulness on their faces. He was so happy for the company but knew his time to leave them was near. His only real concern was Carren. She took him as her grandpa. Will she be able to cope with the lost? He dismissed the idea and decided to cross the bridge when it was time.

Noe was the first to awake of the children and what he saw popped his eyes. It left him speechless. He woke Carren and Yaya, who was still fast asleep next to him. When they awoke and got a glimpse at his face, both sit up with frowns on their faces. Carren, "What's wrong, you look as though you have seen a ghost." All Noe could do was pointing in the direction of the sea.

Now all three were fascinated, as they had never seen anything like this before. A few meters away, stood water upright. Noe wanted to know if what he saw was real and both agreed. Noe whispered, "This God is powerful. Look at the path between the walls of water.'

The next moment they heard Moses' voice as he instructed the families to get up and ready, as the Lord had created a path for them through the sea. The people were amazed at what they saw. Some were sceptic whether the wall of water would last. Within minutes all of them were ready to move through the walls of water.

When the children had to enter the walls of water, they had all forgotten where they were. It was like walking in an aquarium with the fishes above and around you in massive tanks. Noe saw all the fish swimming past, and it was the most significant experience he had, as his grandfather had told him a lot of sea stories and fishes. That's why his dad loves the waters. When he was a bit stressed, they would always pack for a weekend at the coast. His dad would stand for hours fishing, while they would pick mussels or just play and built sandcastles.

Noe wanted to touch the water, but Carren grabbed his hand, reprimanding him just to walk. He looked intense into the water, and it fascinated him. The different species of fish swimming past them and pocked their noses at the wall. It was almost as though the fish was in a big tank, trying to communicate with the people. His dad's fish tank was nothing compared to what he saw here. He put his hand against the water, but it felt protected by a layer of silicon, as his hand wobbled over it. Next, the fish came swimming towards his hand, and they entertained him for quite a while. Noe felt lost in the moment. All he was interested in was the beauty until he was disturbed by the yelling of women.

With a shock, he pulled his hand back and saw how the children surrounded Asaph. He tried to calm them and wondered what caused their fear. When he looked back, he saw the Egyptian army behind them, following them with their chariots and the facial expressions were vicious. As though they wanted to beat them up and took them into captivity again.

But what he also saw, was the nearer the chariots would come, their wheels jammed and couldn't move ahead, some wheels were splashing in all direction. Then men and horse came tumbling down, just for another one overtaking them.

The shouts of some Egyptian men reached Noe's ears, "Let's get away from the Israelites! The Lord is fighting for them against Egypt." But the rest just ignored them and moved on.

Noe started to walk faster. He was almost running, as all the people were in a hurry to get to the other side. It was almost like a stampede was about to take place, as it was the animals, treasures and household goods they had. Some had babies and small children, and Noe saw how families helped one another. They worked together as a team enlightened the burdens of others.

Yaya grabbed their attention as she pointed out that they were about to reach the banks on the other side. The Egyptian army was near and was about to catch up with them.

The Israelites continued moving ahead, and when the last Israelite family set foot on the banks, Moses asked the people to get back. The chariots on full speed chased after them and were just about to reach the banks when Moses lifted his staff.

Before their eyes, the waters came rushed together. The sound was that of many 'waters'. The water flowed back and covered the chariots and horse riders. The sea engulfed the entire army of Pharaoh that had followed the Israelites into the sea. Not one of them survived.

Meantime the hospital janitor had walked his friend back home and when he saw the coast clear. He jumped his bicycle and hurried to Asaph's place, as he knew he missed a lot already, but perhaps he could listen to a story of two. He looked around and saw no one, but lifted the branches and saw the children bicycles hidden. He added his and quickly sneaked off.

When he opened the hedge and crawled through, Missy came licking his face and gave small cries. He looked up and saw no one around and wondered where they were. Perhaps Asaph had shown them his garden, he called, too afraid to shout, as he didn't know who pass and hear his voice. It was Missy drawing his attention as she bit his pants and seemed to pull him in a direction. She left him and ran ahead with him following behind.

Missy stopped in the middle of the garden where the children always sat, and he saw the big book laying with the coin next to it. He knew something went wrong but didn't know what.

He picked the coin and studied it. Missy draw his attention again and put her nose to the book, trying to open it. He sat down and opened the book and Missy pocked her nose to what looked like a place the coin fit. She barked continuously, and he knew he had to slot the coin into the opening.

He placed the coin in the slot and the next moment it seemed as though children came flying through the air.

When the children saw where they were, they ran up to the hospital janitor and hugged him. They were so glad to see him, and he didn't know why. Asaph walked up to him and thanked him and told him everything they went through.

Carren looked at the janitor and tears formed as she thanked him, "if it weren't for you, we would have travelled with the Israelites. Or I don't know what to think. I know we are in big trouble. My parents must be out of their wits looking for me, as I didn't go home." The janitor looked at them with confusion and said, but it was still the same day, he was just an hour late and showed them his time.

Day 6: The Wilderness

School Janitor Recorded The Children

It was Monday, and Carren was glad the weekend was over. All her cousins had a gathering at their place, and they enjoyed one another's company. They always enjoy these moments together. This time they made pizza, and she knew she and little Anna was supposed to win, but Yaya's brother was such a bad loser that her mom decided his group won. They accepted as he was also one of the youngest.

The janitor was back at school and excited to put a recorder underneath the bench Carren and Yaya were always sitting. Before the break, he couldn't wait to reach the bench. He took his broom, along with a bucket of soap water. He waited for all the children to settle in their respected classes and then acted as though he cleaned the bench. He put a small recording device underneath it. His device had the recording ability of at least 30 minutes. It was his uncles, and a bit old and outdated, but at least it worked. He needed proof that they were visiting the psycho in the forest.

The bell rang, and he watched the two girls. He saw Carren headed for the bench and before long, Yaya joined her. He smiled and saw them talking non-stop, and he couldn't wait for the break to finish to listen to the recording.

After the break, when all the children were in class, he ran off to the bench, took the recorder and ran off to his little storeroom. He played the recorder, and all he heard was their cousins' gathering the weekend. Then his attention was gripped as Carren started to tell Yaya of the danger they were in when they got stuck ... and the recorded 30 minutes lapsed. He kicked the boxes in the storeroom, upset. They just about revealed their visits to the forest when this stupid thing died. Angry, he threw the device in his backpack and walked out.

After school, the children knew their routine to the forest and Asaph's cottage.

Missy welcomed them with a wagging tail, and Noe lifted her into his arms, as his family loved dogs. Choco, his dog, a beautiful black Labrador and his favourite. Gentle by heart and very playful.

Carren once again admired the peace of Asaph's place. She wished her parents could buy a getaway cottage near Asaph's, then she could visit him anytime and not just after school. She missed seeing him over the weekend.

Asaph's face lit when he saw the children and waved saying, "I'll be with you in a minute, as I'm finishing your drinks. You can sit, I will join you in a few minutes." Yaya offered to help, but he affirmed he was okay. It was his pleasure to spoil and serve them.

All took their seating position, and Yaya looked at Noe and Carren. Carren immediately knew what she was looking for, and replied, "I've decided to rather keep the book with me as in Noe's hands it means danger."

Noe smiled and dismissed Carren's words with his hand. He saw the hospital janitor coming near with a big smile on his face. He was like a child zoomed in for more.

The next moment all heard a massive explosive voice, almost as though something fell from the sky. All looked into the direction and saw a few meters away, two people standing at a mountain and talk. They immediately knew it was Moses and Aaron. Moses looked tired as he leaned on his staff and spoke to his brother. "Aaron, I don't understand my people. They saw so many good things the Lord had done for us, but still, they forget so easily. They complained by me when the water at Marah was bitter. Then they moaned for bread, because in Egypt they ate better. When the Lord rained the manna, they wanted meat again." Aaron sighed, comforting his brother, as tears ran down Moses's cheeks, "I know my brother. I remember the rock you had to hit to get water. And the Lord gave us the water in abundance to drink."

Both became quiet as they went down and sat, looking over the desert and the people when Moses replied, "they can show at least a bit of gratitude for what the Lord had done for them. They worked so hard as slaves in Egypt, but still they want to go back at times. Look at their clothes and shoes. Still the same. Isn't that enough reason to know that God is at work in their lives?"

Aaron put his hand on Moses's arm and said, "Brother, the moaning of these people will cause you sleepless nights. The Lord hears their every moaning and groaning. He is not deaf. Let's do our part and the Lord his."

Asaph came with the drinks and a basket what looked like bread pieces. They asked him what it was, as it looked like a wafer inside covered with honey. It tasted like wafer chocolate and melted in their mouths. All wanted to know the recipe, as they had never eaten bread with the taste of chocolate.

Asaph smiled and told them it was manna; he picked them up this morning. The children's mouths open and a buzzing noise rose amongst them, wanting to deny the possibility of manna to rain down from heaven. Yaya silent them and told them this was an enchanted garden and anything was possible, as, with God, all things were possible.

They had to agree, as it was beyond good and they craved for more. Next moment soft drops of manna fell from the sky, and there was no need to get up. Each of them just stretched their hands, picked it up and put it to their mouths.

Smiles covered their faces at the taste of it, and when they had enough, they wondered what would happen to the rest laying on the grass, but it soon melted away, and there was no trace of it. The children looked at one another and concluded, their parents and the community should never found out about Asaph's place, as they wouldn't believe what happened here at times. They would destroy Asaph's home because of their ignorance. The times they spend here was memorable, and they didn't know what to expect as things just happened, and it was beautiful.

Asaph sat down with them and took out his book. The children felt much safer with his book than the one Noe had in his hand a couple of days back. The children started to bubble about how rebellious the Israelites were and how they gave Moses headaches. Asaph nodded and agreed, and then said they even built a golden calf as their god.

Noe was the first one to say, "No way, not after all the Lord had done for them." The others agreed, and within minutes they were in-depth discussion of how the Israelites could betray the Lord like that.

Asaph let them reason and then told them he would read the story from his big book. "When the people saw that Moses took long in coming down the mountain, they gathered around Aaron and said, "Come, make us gods who will go before us. As for this fellow Moses, who brought us up out of Egypt, we don't know what has happened to him."

Aaron answered them, "Take off the gold earrings that your wives, your sons and your daughters are wearing, and bring them to me." So all the people took off their earrings and brought them to Aaron. He took what they handed him and made it into a 'god' cast in the shape of a calf and fashioning it with a tool. Then they said, "This is our god, who brought you up out of Egypt."

The children gasped and were upset. "How dare they make a golden cow their god. We just ate manna. He gave them and what about the plagues he sent throughout Egypt, did they forget about that? And what about the red sea we travelled through on dry foot. Couldn't they see the wonders of God?

"That cow can do nothing! Human hands made it, and our hands cannot create a god. Just look around, all these God created, by just speaking it into existence. How stupid these people can be."

Asaph looked at the children and said it still happens in today's life. People had little ornaments made of stone, wood, copper, silver, gold and various substances and treated those things as their God. Some were so ignorant; they didn't even know they were busy with idolatry. It was a bad custom passed down from one generation to another.

Asaph continued with his reading, "When Aaron saw this, he built an altar in front of the calf and announced, "Tomorrow there will be a festival to the Lord." So the next day, the people rose early and sacrificed burnt offerings and presented fellowship offerings. Afterwards, they sat down to eat and drink and got up to indulge in festivities.

Asaph looked up from the book and locked the children eyes and said, "The Lord knew all along what they were busy doing. He instructed Moses to go down because his people he brought up out of Egypt, had become corrupt." The Lord further told Moses,

"They have been quick to turn away from what I commanded them and have made themselves an idol cast in the shape of a calf. They have bowed down to it and sacrificed to it and have said, "These are your gods, Israel, who brought you up out of Egypt."

Asaph continued and told them about David, a man so near Gods' heart also spoke about the idols of people made with silver and gold. And they were made by human hands. They had mouths, but couldn't speak, eyes, but couldn't see, ears, but couldn't hear. And noses, but couldn't smell. Their hands couldn't even feel, and it couldn't walk nor utter a sound. The Lord wants us to trust in him and only him.

The children wanted to know what the Lord said about all these gods that the Israelites made and wanted to incline it was Him. Asaph looked down to his book and read what the Lord thought of it all.

"I have seen these people," the Lord said to Moses, "and they are a stiff-necked people. Now leave me alone so that my anger may burn against them and that I may destroy them. Then I will make you into a great nation."

Asaph looked up from his book and said, "Moses was upset when he came down and saw the people had built a golden calf. He dropped the tablets the

Lord wrote with His finger. The law the Lord gave to his children."

Moses then called those who were faithful to the Lord aside and instructed them to kill those who believed in the god they made with their hands. About 3000 Israelites died that day.

The children looked at one another, and a buzzing noise arose amongst them as they realized the seriousness of such an offence. If you want to make scarifies to a god made by human hands.

Carren gently asked a question, "Was the Lord pleased with what Moses had done to the people; it sounds so weird killing your own people."

Asaph replied, "The Lord wanted to destroy all of them, but Moses asked the Lord to pardon them, as what would the Egyptians think of their God destroying the very people he freed from Egypt."

Yaya replied that Moses and the Lord had a good relationship. She wondered if he had ever seen the Lord face to face because she knew her Sunday school teacher said if you see God face to face, you will die.

Asaph nodded his head and said, Moses wanted to see the glory of the Lord because the Lord told him He was pleased with him, and Yaya is right. The Lord further said to Moses that He would cause all his goodness to pass in front of Moses, and he would proclaim his name, the Lord in front of Moses' presence. The Lord further announced He would have mercy on whom He would have mercy and compassion on whom he would have compassion, but Moses couldn't saw His face, for no one might saw him and live. But the Lord told Moses he would place him in a nearby cliff and pass by.

Next, the children's hearts trembled with fear when they heard a voice from heaven proclaiming, "The Lord, the Lord, the compassionate and gracious God..." the voice trailed away. The children looked up, waiting for what would happen next when they saw word lines gently coming down. Once in their hands, they realized it was a message from God and one by one, the children started to read what was in their hands.

Carren was the first to read hers, "The Lord is slow to anger," Yaya continued, "abounding in love and faithfulness." Noe said, and mine read, "Maintaining love to thousands." The janitor held up his and proclaimed, "and forgiving wickedness, rebellion and sin."

That means, no one will ever be punished the children uttered, but those still sitting with the sentence words disagreed and started to read theirs.

"Yet he does not leave the guilty unpunished."

"He punishes the children and their children for the sin of the parents to the third and fourth generation."

When the children heard the last sentence, they started to argue and said it was unfair. Why should they be punished for their parents and grandparents sin even to the fourth generation?

Asaph calmed them down and replied that they should remember... and before he could continue, they heard the most loving, gentle voice within their mist.

"My nature is love, so I am slow to anger and abounding in love and faithfulness." The children simultaneously touched their cheeks and proclaimed, it was almost as though the words brushed past their cheeks. Their hearts instantly filled with admiration for what just happened, and they remembered that the Lord is and will always be love.

"The Lord is slow to anger," Yaya continued, "abounding in love and faithfulness."

Yaya continued and told the children for forty years the Israelites wandered in the desert, without their clothes or shoes worn out. The children shook their heads and replied it was impossible. Their clothes and shoes needed replacement every year or two like ours. Sometimes we replace our school clothes twice a year.

Noe replied, "Forty years, that would be impossible. The baby's clothes they had on when they left Egypt, their small booties or shoes. How would they fit in it after forty years? That would be impossible. That cannot be true."

The children agreed, and Asaph had to intervene and said Yaya was right, the Lord said in His word the Israelites clothes did not wear out.

Their feet never got swollen during the forty years. And there were skilled women amongst them who spun fine linen from goat hair. Those time they made clothes, past smaller clothes down to siblings, but what stood fast, was their clothes didn't wither.

Noe nodded his head and agreed what Asaph said made sense. That would be more like it. He continued to reason by saying, if the Lord could create heaven and earth, he could let shoes become bigger or smaller, make garments grow on the children. That could also have been.

All the children agreed with Noe and continued discussing the topic until it was time for them to leave.

Day 7: The Promise Land

The Janitor Took Photos

The school janitor hasted to the forest before the children came from school and hid nearby the bench he had a chat with the hospital janitor. Today would be the day he would expose whatever and whoever they met in the forest.

One by one the children past, and as Carren dropped her bicycle, she sensed someone watching her. She looked up, and her eyes pierced the forest trees in search of what or whose eyes she felt on her.

The school janitor drew his head just in time. His heart pounded at the thought of being caught. He hoped the girl wouldn't walk to where he hid. She would derail his plans. She can be very outspoken and would make a scene. He came this far; he wouldn't like anyone to saw him spying on them. He held his breath and then heard crackling leaves as the girl's steps indicated that she was on the move.

He peaked, just on time, and saw her opening a hedge of trees and disappeared. A big smile covered his face. Today would be the day he'll expose them. He knew they were up to mischief.

He sneaked near and heard a voice talking to the children. He started to feel for the opening where she got in, but couldn't find it and then heard the bark of a dog. He jumped back and hid until the coast was clear. He ran to the hiding spot of Carren's bicycle and saw about ten or more bikes hidden. He gave a big smile, took a picture and ran home, ready to inform the parents

Asaph looked at Missy, and he frowned. Then Missy stopped barking, and he was relieved and continued telling the story that Moses was old, and the Lord had shown him the Promised Land and then took him to be with Him. Before Moses went to be with the Lord, he laid his hands on Joshua, who became the new leader of the Israelites.

Asaph continued that Joshua was one of the twelve spies Moses had sent to the Promised Land, where it overflowed with milk and honey. The grapes were massive, and everything was bigger and in abundance. Moses sent twelve spies to speculate the land, Canaan. He instructed them to go through the Negev and then into the mountain region.

Suddenly a simulation popped and they saw twelve men sitting with Moses, and a plan was in front of them. The children struggled to peek in as to see what it was about, but they couldn't see. The next moment the entire map lifted in front of them – it was massive. As the men discussed an invisible pen marked the path they should take.

Noe was the first one to respond, "Wow that is cool. I wish I could go with them; look, dressed like real spies. Look at them, always on the lookout and alert who's listening or watching to them."

The children were intrigued by the journey the men had to take to investigate the land. Moses's in a clear voice, instructed the twelve to see what the land was like and whether the people were strong or weak and their totals. Each spy took out an old fashioned paper, it looked like a scroll and wrote down the instructions and hid it in a holder, slotting it next to their sides. They wrote down all they had to do, as Moses instructed them to see if the land those people lived in was good or bad. Were the cities surrounded by walls or not and they should look at the soil, whether it was rich or poor. If trees were present how it looked and he also ordered them to bring along some fruit for them to observe the quality thereof.

The twelve nodded, greeted their families and off they went in the direction Moses instructed.

Then the scene disappeared, and it was almost as though someone broadcasted their journey live. The children were able to track all the spies and was relieved when they heard they reached the land. They hold their breath, as the radio presenter informed them they were all in the city now. A few heads turned and looked intense at a spy, almost as to say he didn't belong there, but then dismissed the idea and walked on.

The children relieved to hear they got to the city and blended in with the rest of the population. However, they at times looked tiny, as a lot of tall people were present in the city.

The reporter stopped, and the children's faces were in expectancy as to what happened to them in the city.

Asaph told them they were in the city for about forty days and returned to the camp and reported to Moses, Aaron and the rest of the Israelites. They brought a big bunch of grapes and had to carry it on a pole showing how big their fruit was. They even brought some pomegranates and figs.

They reported to Moses the land was flowing with milk and honey, but the walls were huge.

Joshua and Caleb had useful positive reports, but the other ten spies said they couldn't attack those people, as they were too strong. They started to spread lies among the Israelites about the land they had explored. They said the land devoured those living there. They told the people they looked like grasshoppers amongst the people.

Asaph sigh and Carren wanted to know what was wrong. Was he tired, did he need some rest, but he shook his head, telling them the Lord was on the verge of punishing the Israelites again because they started moaning and groaning again.

Noe shouted, "They've learned that manners from the Egyptians. Pharaoh and his people were also so hardheaded. Perhaps they've stayed too long with those people and adopted their ways."

Yaya replied, "It can be, as sometimes we are friends with the wrong children, the naughty ones, and also become like them. My dad always says, 'show me your friends, and I will tell you who you are."

The children started reasoning and said, but it's not true. Their parents are judging other children. Some of their friends are just a little bit naughty, but not much. They just steal the children's lunch.

Carren reprimanded them all and argued that those children start small, by taking something that doesn't belong to them, so it was stealing. Later on, they'll get into the habit of stealing bigger things, as they got into a pattern of taking what doesn't belong to them.

Noe agreed and reminded them of the Lord's words on the second day they visited Asaph. He said we shouldn't steal. But it is then such a small steal, why would it be such a big thing? Would stealing bread be the same as stealing a car? And what if the child was hungry?

All agreed with Noe. Stealing bread and stealing a car was different sins. How could you be punished the same way for both?

Asaph saw where the conversation was heading to and gently told them, whatever they took that didn't belong to them, was stealing. Big or small - it was stealing.

"Okay, got it," Noe replied. They wanted to continue with the debate when they heard the deep, but gentle voice of the Lord and instantly all looked from where it came. As the voice spoke, the clouds made sentences above them, and all listened and read simultaneously.

"Joshua, son of Nun, Moses' assistant, Moses my servant is dead. Now then, you and all these people, get ready to cross the Jordan River into the land I am about to give them - the Israelites. I will give you every place where you set your foot, as I promised Moses. Your territory will extend from the desert to Lebanon, and from the great river, the Euphrates - all the Hittite country - to the Mediterranean Sea west. No one will be able to stand against you all the days of your life. As I was with Moses, so I will be with you; I will never leave you nor forsake you. Be strong and courageous, because you will lead these people to inherit the land I swore to their ancestors to give them.

Be strong and very courageous. Be careful to obey all the law my servant Moses gave you; do not turn from it to the right or the left that you may be successful wherever you go. Keep this Book of the Law always on your lips; meditate on it day and night, so that you may be careful to do everything written in it. Then you will be prosperous and successful. Have I not commanded you? Be strong and courageous. Do not be afraid; do not be discouraged, for the Lord, your God will be with you wherever you go."

Yaya was the first to reply, "Oh, so sweet. The Lord loves Joshua to talk to him like that." Why can't I hear the voice of the Lord like that?"

Carren answered, "Yaya, but you just did."

The children started with questions of what happened to Moses, and why he didn't lead the people to the Promised Land.

Carren told them that Moses was already old, and they had to fight to get the land the Lord promised them. So the people needed someone young and fresh. Remember he was one of the spies with the positive report.

The hospital Janitor shared, almost as in disbelief, "All these years working at the hospital, I was so afraid to get the diseases from people hospitalized and thought I would die. I would wash and scrub till five times and more when I came from certain wards. Afraid to die. During the night, I would get nightmares of catching a virus and die. Now I heard these beautiful, self-assured words of the Lord with new ears, 'I will never leave you nor forsake you."

He rubbed his hands, and happiness was visible on his face when he said, "I will write these words on my cupboard, and would meditate on it daily for strength. Fear and nightmares will no longer be part of my life!" Asaph agreed and ensure him the Lord never slumber nor sleep.

The children replied, "Wow, the Lord is going to battle with them. If He is with them, they won't lose a battle."

Asaph agreed and continued telling the story. He said to them that Joshua had sent two spies to Jericho to observe and report what was going on there. They went straight to a prostitute Rahab's house and stayed there. The...

Noe was surprised, "There were prostitutes in the bible? That's a first. Why would they go there?"

Asaph nonchalant continue, as to say they knew she would help them and she did. The king found out about the two strange men in the city and sent his soldiers to Rahab's house to look for them. She was quick on her feet and hid them on the roof and told the kings men a lie, as to say they were there, but left. The pursuers went from her place to look for the men, but couldn't find them.

Carren listened to Asaph, but thoughts of Rahab came to her, what if the king found she lied? He would have killed her. It was as though seeing Rahab walking up and down after the pursuers left. She was wondering what she should do, as she had heard a lot of stories of the Israelites. Instantly she made up her mind and thought, she will negotiate her freedom with them. She helped them, so they owe her a favour in return.

Asaph saw Carren captured in her thoughts with a frown between the eyes and wanted to know what she was thinking.

She told them, she was thinking of Rahab, if she wanted something in return, for hiding the spies as the king would have killed her if he knew about her lies.

Asaph smiled and replied, "Yes, Rahab, went up to the spies and told them, she knew the Lord had given them Jericho. She also said how fearful she and her family were. She continued to share, an entire fear had fallen on the inhabitants of Jericho and they are melting in fear of the Israelites coming their way."

Rahab told them, all in Jericho heard how the Lord dried up the water of the Red Sea when they came from Egypt. And what they had done in Sihon and Og and how they had destroyed those two kings. She continued that the entire population's hearts melted in fear and everyone's courage had failed as the Israelites God was the God in heaven above and on the earth below.

One of the children wanted to know if sinners also know the works of God. It seemed as though sinners lived without fear of the Lord, now why did the people of Jericho fear?

Noe replied, "Wouldn't you fear if you knew these people had a God, which help them destroy kings and gave their land to them? Come-on, get real. And now you heard and knew these people were on their way to your city."

All the children agreed and said they would have fled to another town but would lock down their city, as those days they had the big gates in front of their cities.

Carren agreed and had taken out her book, as to read, as the children were asking too many questions. She wanted to know what the outcome was and what had happened to Rahab.

Asaph looked at Carren. Her attention focused on the open book in front of her. Asaph was surprised at how she found the passage so quickly. Without a further word, he asked her to continue reading what Rahab had done.

Carren started reading the passage, but as she opened her mouth, her voice changed, and she sounded more like a young woman. The other's eyes lifted, but they didn't say a word.

"Please swear to me by the Lord that you will show kindness to my family because I have shown kindness to you." She took a deep breath and continued, "Give me a sure sign that you will spare the lives of my father and mother, my brothers and sisters, and all who belong to them – and that you will save us from death."

There was a long pause of silence. Noe sitting next to Carren continued reading, almost as though the spies had to make up their minds, as Rahab wanted her entire families, saved. All who belong to her.

Noe in a deep men's voice, "Our lives for your lives! If you don't tell what we are doing, we will treat you kindly and faithfully when the Lord gives us the land."

Carren had a smile on her face when she continued reading in a voice that was not her own. The children knew it was the voice of Rahab; she had a sweet, gentle voice, one you would easily believe and help at the same time.

Carren, "Come, this rope is strong enough to let you down through the window, down the city wall. Please go to the hills for the pursuers not to find you. Hide yourselves there three days until they return, and then go on your way."

Noe, instantly continued in a deep voice, "This oath you made with us - swear will not be binding on us, unless, when we enter the land, you have tied this scarlet cord in the window through which you let us down. And unless you have brought your father and mother, your brothers and all your family into your house.

If any of them go outside your house into the street, their blood will be on their heads. We will not be responsible. As for those who are in the house with you - their blood will be on our head if a hand is laid on them."

Noe kept his breath, and the silence became tangible. He continued talking again, "But if you tell what we are doing, we will not be responsible for keeping the oath by which we swore."

Carren replied, "Agreed! Let it be as you say."

The children wanted to know what happened to the spies and Rahab.

Asaph told them, the spies reached the camp safely and told Joshua how afraid the people were of them. Their Lord had certainly given Jericho into their hands.

Noe smiled and looked at Carren, and she knew he was again up to something.

"What?" asked Carren?

Noe with the smile Carren knew so well, "Can't we spin the coin to see what happened to Jericho? But you can spin it. I will keep my hands off the coin, promise."

Carren looked at Asaph, and he agreed, and Noe's face lit with excitement. Everything will be live again.

Carren took the coin from the book and tried to spin it, but every time it fell flat before she could flick it. Noe wanted to grab the coin and showed Carren how it worked, but she covered it with her hand, reprimanding him as not to touch the coin. In his hands, it was a danger.

The children agreed, and Yaya offered to flick the coin. She knew how to flick a coin, as she and her brothers always competed with one another of whose coin spun the longest. She usually won, as she was the eldest. She took the coin from Carren and twisted it. Instantly a simulation appeared, and they saw the Israelites preparing themselves to cross the Jordan River.

The children looked as though it was a movie they watched. They observed when the Ark was on the move, the people followed it. Still, then they saw a river flowing and heard the commotion of the people asking Joshua how they should cross the Jordan River. He told them to follow the Ark of the Covenant as he knew the Lord promised to exalt him. The people followed the Ark, and the children could see that people were gossiping how Joshua would get them to pass the Jordan River.

Suddenly the scenery changed and they were in a town, Adam. The children ran home to call their parents to look at the strange phenomena. The river that was once in flood stood in a heap and didn't flow down the river. The river bed was dry, and the people started to panic. The children's' eyes popped, as they looked at the water, heaped together. It was as though someone had gathered the water like a heap of sand and brought it along.

Asaph and the children smiled and knew it was the hand of the Lord, as nothing was impossible to the Lord. He once parted the Red Sea with them plotting along. So God could do it again. The people near the river, watched the strange phenomena, started to grab their children's' hands and ran in the opposite direction. The fear amongst them was tangible.

The scenery moved back to the Jordan River still in full flood and the priests busy carrying the Ark. The men continued with their walk, and as soon as their feet touched the water, it gave way, and the ground was visible. A sheer went up, and some people fell to their knees and worshipped the Lord.

Some men in uniform saw the Israelites crossing the Jordan River on dry ground, jumped from their lookout point to inform their king what happened.

Here and their men fell, and the children wondered why, until Yaya pointed out it must be fear. The children agreed, as they knew at times when they were afraid, it seemed as though their legs became lame. And Yaya added, Rahab told the spies how fearful the people of Jericho were.

The men ran into Jericho and informed the king. Fear arose on all the faces, as the king ordered them to close the gates, as no one would get in, neither get out. People started running in all directions and bolt their doors. The fear was so tangible that Carren and the children were on the edge themselves.

Then they saw trails of dust within a distance and knew it was the Israelites on their way to Jericho, but Carren wanted to know, how they would get in, as the walls were thick and high. Look at the bolts around their gates. And on the walls, the armed men had taken their positions.

The girls didn't want to look, as they will start to fight, as soon as the Israelites were near. But to their surprise, they heard the known voice and looked up. They saw Joshua nodded his head and knew the Lord was in conversation with him.

The children overheard the conversation, "Joshua, see, I have delivered Jericho into your hands, along with its king and its fighting men. March around the city once with all the armed men. Do this for six days. Have seven priests carry trumpets of rams' horns in front of the Ark. On the seventh day, march around the city seven times, with the priests blowing the trumpets. When you hear them sound a long blast on the trumpets, have the whole army give a loud shout; then the wall of the city will collapse, and the army will go up, everyone straight in."

The Israelite armed men walked around Jericho and inside the walls, the people had their own stories of what they were doing outside. From the hall they heard the kings' fighting men said, the Israelites walked around the wall, looking for a place to enter, but their gates tightly shut, no one will ever enter.

Most people were afraid but found their courage in the strength of the gates. Then they saw Rahab running over the plains, collecting all her family. She was in serious talk, and they remembered the bargain she made with the two spies. Yaya whispered, "What a smart deal. Clever girl. Who said girls couldn't think."

"Quiet, as nobody should talk while walking around the city."

They saw the Israelites walked around the city, and the children wondered what would happen. Inside the walls, you could sense the peoples' fear, as they didn't know what their opponent was doing. The Israelite men marched around the city, with the seven priests in front of them, blowing on their horns. By the seventh time, a long sound of the horns blew, and the entire army gave a loud shout. It was loud! Goosebumps hit the children's' bodies, as fear gripped their hearts. All seemed so real, as though they were there—even the people inside the city walls, scattered.

The children saw this massive right hand, pressing down on the wall, it looked endless, and then they heard and noticed the crack sound of the walls as though ignited with dynamite. The walls of Jericho came tumbling down. People surprised at what just happened, shouted, "I told you their God was fighting along with them." Others tried to get away, searching for a hiding place.

The Israelites army charged straight in, their swords drawn, ready to fight.

The girls shouted, "Yaya, put back the coin. We don't want to see the fight."

Yaya obeyed and slotted the coin to its place, and everything became as calm as before. The boys wanted more, but Asaph told them to read the rest at home, as it was getting late. All who watched the walls tumbled were in awe and excited about what God could do. To think they just walked around the city walls, blown the horns, shouted together and the walls came down. Amazed by the greatness of God, they applauded the God of the universe. They wanted Asaph to tell them more warfare stories and wanted to know how many kings Joshua destroyed and cities the twelve tribes took as their possession.

Asaph told them Joshua was a brave warrior; he and his army concurred thirty-one kings.

Carren wanted to know what happened to Rahab and her family. Asaph told her they were all saved and were taken in by the Israelites. The girls wanted to be smart like Rahab, protecting and saving their entire family. In contrast, the boys wanted to be Joshua's.

The way he stood up straight, how he planned, the faith in the Lord and how he concurred city after city. They were moving fearlessly from one town to the other.

Carren thought, Rahab was brave, she needed to share the story with others, as girls also featured in the great book as heroes, but she wanted to know how they would do it. Yaya excitedly introduced the plan, "We should wear scarlet red ribbons to school. I know the girls would want to know why the ribbons. Then we can tell them the story of Rahab's bravery." The girls embraced the plan and Asaph looked at them and felt happiness overwhelmed his heart.

Asaph quickly turned away to hid his tears of gladness, smiled and gave all a fresh glass of berry juice. The children felt overwhelmed and wanted to stay longer, but they knew they had to leave.

At home Carren, Noe and Yaya's parents were together when the janitor came in. He didn't even greeted them properly when informing the parents that their children were talking to an older man deep in the forest. The parents somewhat irritable, because of his lack of manners wanted to dismiss the idea, when he took his phone and showed them the bicycles piled up together.

Carren's mom laughed and said the children were just exploring the forest. And reprimanded him for following their children, but she'll ask her daughter where she was when she came home.

When Carren got home, her mom told her about the school janitor and his visit, but she dismissed it as she knew they loved the forest. Carren smiled and assured her mom; they were just exploring a bit. She then knew they should be careful, as she sensed someone present in the forest earlier.

Day 8: Captivity

The Janitor Led the Parents to the Old Man

The next day, the school janitor decided to go to the forest ahead of the children. He would hide near the entrance he saw the children went in and took pictures of them behind the hedge

The day before he was disturbed, but he heard voices and even a dog barked. He paved his way to the spot where he saw Carren disappeared and slid in and hid behind one of the hedges, awaiting the children to come.

He didn't wait long before hearing bicycles dropped and the low whispers of children. If he was not mistaken, his friends' voice was amongst the children. He dismissed the idea as his friend would never side himself with them.

The janitor moved deeper and was just a few meters from where the children entered, and he held his breath, not to be noticed by the children.

Noe was the first one to mention a strong perfume smell and wanted to know whether Yaya and Carren could smell it. They all agreed and wanted to know whose perfume it was, as it belonged to an adult.

The school janitor sat frozen, knowing if the children start following the scent, they will find him. He didn't even think his cologne was that strong. He sat on the edge, as the children started to follow the scent.

Noe, was about to uncover his hiding spot when Carren told him it was their friend the hospital janitor. He laughed and said it was his cologne with the strong smell.

Noe dropped the leaves and turned around. The school janitor wiped his sweat and was relieved. A frown popped between his eyes, as he realised it was his friend's voice he heard. He was also the one giving him the cologne as a birthday gift because his friend loved the scent on him - traitor! Fury raised in the school janitor's heart when he realised his friend betrayed him. Today is the day he will expose them all.

It seemed as though his friend was the last one to the entrance. He quickly neared the place, put his camera lens in and just randomly started to take pictures. He couldn't see a thing, as he was too afraid to look, but he knew there was some activity taking place behind the hedge.

He quickly made his way out and marked the place. He couldn't wait to leave the forest, too afraid someone would find him there. He turned right at a designated footpath, as he knew there was a bench. He was eager to see what he has captured.

His hands were shaking as he picked the camera and started to look at what he captured. He saw the first picture and was overwhelmed, at what he saw. A bearded old man walked towards the children. He continued looking at the photos, and everything seemed so unreal. It was a beauty he had never seen before. Thus, the stories of the psycho of the forest were real. He was excited. He felt proud of himself, as all this time, all made him look crazy, while they were visiting someone.

He will quickly visit a few parents he knew would like to hunt down the psycho and show them the place. They should just be careful and let the children be safe, as he could harm the children if he knew the parents were on their way.

Asaph saw the children enter and the always broad smile welcomed them. He was ready with their refreshing drink and the children ever wondered how he could make the drinks he made. He told them he'd take them on ta tour through his entire garden after his storytelling session soon.

Carren, as usual, stepped up and hugged him and told him he was the best thing happening to her. She always wanted to visit and would like him to meet her parents. They'll understand as her mother loved older people.

Asaph gave Carren's refreshing drink and turned around - his eyes troubled. He knew he had to tell her his assignment was coming to an end, and he wanted to go home. His home was where his Father was. She took a glimpse of his troubled eyes and took his hand and squeezed it. Affirming him that all would be fine, things would work out for the best to all of them.

All the children positioned themselves on the grass, and Asaph started telling them about Jeremiah a boy their age who the Lord appointed to talk to His people. Noe was the first one to ask if they could see the visual thing. He promised he would keep his hands to himself.

Asaph permitted them to do so. Noe stretched his hand to take the coin, and all shouted "no". He smiled and told them he joked with them. Yaya reached for the coin and spun it.

Instantly they saw the boy and knew it must be Jeremiah talking to himself, "I'm a child how would these adults and elders listen to me. I do not know how to speak."

They saw a cloud moving, and next heard that familiar voice who had spoken to them before.

The Lord spoke to Jeremiah, "Do not say, "I am only a child." You must go to everyone I send you to and say whatever I command you. Do not be afraid of them, for I am with you and will rescue you."

They saw a hand moved and touched the boy's lips. "Now, I have put my words in your mouth. See today I appoint you over nations and kingdoms to uproot and to pull down, to destroy and overthrow, to build and to plant."

The children simultaneously said, "Wow, that's cool. Just imagine telling our parents when they do wrong."

The children wanted to know more about the status of a prophet and Asaph told them it was a spokesperson for the Lord.

The children were still in discussion when they heard the intensity in the Lord's voice. "Go and tell My people, I remember the devotion of your youth, how, as a bride, you loved me and followed me through the wilderness. ... What fault did your fathers find in me, that they strayed so far from me? They followed worthless idols and became worthless themselves. They did not ask for me.

I brought them into a fertile land to eat its fruit and abundant produce."

Then the children saw a scroll falling, and written in a strange language. They looked at one another, but all a sudden, a finger moved over the words. As the finger moved, the words changed to English, and the children started to read, "How can you say, "I am not defiled; I have not run after the Baal's...They, their kings and their officials, their priests and their prophets. They say to wood, "You are my father, and to stone, "You gave me birth." They have turned their backs to me and not their faces; yet when they are in trouble, they say, "Come and save us."

Next, all the images of their hand made gods appeared in front of the children. It was almost as though they could touch it and an evil presence of fear gripped their hearts. It was carvings in various sizes, and the children saw how people folded their hands in prayer and went on the knees worshipping those gods.

Fear struck their hearts when they saw a fire from heaven came down and consumed all those images. It was almost as though a mouth of fire opened and swallowed them all.

Then the people ran and made more. They saw the gods on every high hill and under every spreading tree. For hours they carved and said, "oh my god, you are my god. Bent down before these handmade gods and brought an offering to it."

Yaya disappointedly uttered, "How could they forget what the Lord had done? He created them and led them to freedom. He was their cloud by day and fire by night. Did they forget?

They heard a voice almost like in anguish, "Return, faithless Israel...Only acknowledge your guilt – you have rebelled against the Lord your God, you have scattered your favours to foreign gods...O Jerusalem, wash the evil from your hearts and be saved...A besieging army is coming from a distant land, raising a war cry against the cities of Judah. They surround her like men guarding a field, because she has rebelled against me," declares the Lord.

The children saw the prophet Jeremiah sitting with his hands in his hair. He whispered, "If only they have listened to the word of the Lord they wouldn't have been taken into captivity by the king of Babylon for seventy years. But the Lord had mercy on them and promised he would again come for them and bring them back and restore them.

"For I know the plans I have for you," declares the Lord, "plans to prosper you and not to harm you, plans to give you hope and a future. Then you will call upon me and come and pray to me, and I will listen to you. You will seek me and find me when you seek me with all your heart. You will found me," declares the Lord.

The children faces lit up when they heard the last part. So the Lord has plans to prosper us and not to harm us.

Yaya thought out loud, "The Lord is so merciful with his people, did you see the gods they made and worshipped. How could they, after all, the Lord had done for them?"

Noe interrupted, "but I've seen some of those gods in a few houses I visited, but they believe in God and go to church weekly."

The children agreed and told all when they went on holiday in other countries; they brought along those small tokens as a remembrance of the country they visited. Would those be gods?

Asaph nodded his head and agreed. Not all of them though, but it can at times be very deceiving gifts, without being aware that it angers the Lord, as he is a jealous god.

While the children were hanging to Asaph's lips, the school janitor had shown the community where their children were. All saw the old beard man and were up and arms to bring the psycho of the forest to justice. It was by time they capture him, but they should first get their children to safety.

Carren asked Asaph if she could pose a question, but it was a bit off the current discussion. He assured her she could ask him anything.

Carren, "I'm interested to know more about the Old Testament and the New Testament. How do they merge as in the one they spoke about God or Lord all the time and in the New Testament about Jesus?"

Asaph looked at Carren and was glad she asked such a question. And he started to unfold the story. The Lord so loved the world that He decided to give his only son to the world.

Remember Rahab who helped the spies? The children nodded, and Asaph told them the genealogy of Jesus. He came from a bloodline in the Old Testament. Jesus was called the son of David, the son of Abraham.

The genealogy was from Abraham to Isaac to Jacob to Judah...Salmon the father of Boaz, whose mother was Rahab...

Carren was excited when she interrupted Asaph, "Rahab that helped the spies? So Jesus came from her bloodline. Wow, that interesting. Girls just think she and her family were the only surviving ones. She played her cards so well that she married and 'thee' Jesus, the great teacher and miracle worker, came from Rahab's family tree." She continued to bubble and wished her name was Rahab.

The children started to laugh, as some wanted to be Joshua, Caleb, and each one wanted to pick a name.

Asaph continued... Boaz the father of Obed, to Jesse to David. David was called a man after God's own heart. David was the father of Solomon.

Noe interrupted and wanted to know if it was Solomon, the guy who asked for wisdom. Asaph agreed, and Noe continued that he always wanted to be Solomon, because Solomon was very clever and very rich.

The children dismissed Noe's words and told him; he was Noe. Noe from the town of Finelando.

Asaph lightly reprimanded the children. He told them Jesus came from a small town called Nazareth, and when people heard that, they asked the question, "Can anything good come from Nazareth?" They also undermined his strength and the fact that he was their

Saviour. So Noe can become a Solomon in his lifetime, as nothing was impossible for God.

The hospital janitor wanted to know why God called David, a man so after His heart.

Asaph told them, King David loved the Lord; he was always ready to worship him and was passionate to sit at the Lord's feet. He had a servant heart and the Lord look at the heart of people.

David was looking after his father's sheep, when the prophet anointed him as king, to shepherd the Lord's people, with the integrity of heart; with skilful hands, David led them. He was a great warrior, but the stories of David would be for a day on its own.

Suddenly, they heard the sung of birds, and they looked in the direction and saw sparrows sitting on a hedge and made out the number fourteen. The children found it strange and said there must be a message in as sparrows won't just sit in that formation.

Asaph agreed and continued with the genealogy of Jesus and told them there were fourteen generations in all from Abraham to David, fourteen from David to the exile to Babylon, and fourteen from the exile to the Messiah. After Asaph had said that, the sparrows flew off.

Asaph continued and said, "Centuries back, a Saviour has been born; he is the Messiah, the Lord - his name, Jesus!

Conclusion

Tell the Next Generation

Before Asaph could say another word, people came rushing through the hedge, and each parent grabbed their child and marched them to the fence, while the men started to pull on Asaph.

Carren's mom was upset to see her daughter and was overwhelmed that she wasn't hurt. All the parents wanted to know if their children were okay and the children tried to explain that Asaph was a good man.

Carren burst in tears when she heard the weariness in Asaph's voice, and her heart was in pain. How could they harass someone so gentle? She knew she should help him, as she was the one bringing all the children here.

The parents steered them through the opening of the hedge. Once outside, they were marched off by their parents in the direction of their homes.

They could hear the harshness of the men towards Asaph. They literally screamed.

Carren closed her eyes and knew Asaph would never make it. He was too old and frail. Didn't the men have any mercy? It's an old man they are busy tormenting.

At once, she pulled lose and started to run. She ducked through the hedge, and Asaph's eyes met hers and lit up. She passed all the men who held on to him, and she insisted that they leave him. The men tried to block her, but she ducked past them and grabbed the hem of Asaph's garment.

As soon as she did that, he smiled, and his eyes filled with happiness when he whispered, "Carren, thank you for coming here. My time had come, I have to go."

A cloud came down. Men scattered away from Asaph, almost as though hit out of the way. Holiness surrounded him. The cloud moved under his feet and then she saw Missy came running and got on the cloud with Asaph. The cloud started to lift him. From his garment, he took a scroll and dropped it in Carren's hands. She caught it and hid it inside her jacket pocket.

The men still lying on the grass, looked amazed as Asaph was taken up by a cloud and disappeared. The shock was visible on their faces when next, they heard the rumbling sound of destruction.

They looked up and saw the house crumbled to pieces and trees uprooted. She just heard, "run". And all of them started to run for the hedge. The entire place crumbled down, leaving no trace of someone ever living there.

Carren was the last one out and looked over her shoulder and saw the big words appearing where the house once stood. "PSALM 78 - TELL THE NEXT GENERATION THE PRAISEWORTHY DEEDS OF THE LORD, HIS POWER, AND THE WONDERS HE HAS DONE." In the run, Carren nodded and knew she had an assignment and curiously wondered what was written on the scroll.

There was a commotion outside, and all wanted to know what happened. The men walked with bended heads and felt ashamed of what they did as they told the parents what they saw. For all these years, people believed a psycho lived in the forest, but it seemed as though he was a man of God.

All walked home in silence and Carren couldn't wait to get up the attic and be alone. She wanted to read the scroll Asaph gave her.

At home, she told her mom she wanted to be alone. Her mom apologised for being so hard on her, but if she feels, she can share Asaph's stories.

Alone, Carren opened the scroll and saw two messages rolled together. The first one read,

Dear Carren,

By the time you are reading this letter, I would be home.

You and your friends were the best things ever happening to me in a long time. I couldn't go home to my Father, as I had a mission to complete.

The residents for many decades or centuries believed I was someone bad, but you dared to sit at my feet and listen. Thank you for your love. It carried me through these last days. It was memorable, and I would never forget it.

Tell Yaya, Noe and the rest, I send my greetings, and I love them as my own.

But you little girl was special.

Love,

Asaph

Tears ran down Carren's face, but they were tears of joy.

She wiped her face and took the second scroll and saw it was a bit lengthy, but what she immediately saw, was the same words she saw when she ran from his place.

"Psalm 78, A maskil of Asaph." Carren read the passaged and stopped, looked up and made a promise to Asaph that she would tell the next generation. She started to continue reading.

Psalm 78

A *maskil* of Asaph.

¹My people, hear my teaching;
    listen to the words of my mouth.
²I will open my mouth with a parable;
    I will utter hidden things, things from of old—
³things we have heard and known,
    things our ancestors have told us.
⁴We will not hide them from their descendants;
    we will tell the next generation
the praiseworthy deeds of the LORD,
    his power, and the wonders he has done.
⁵He decreed statutes for Jacob
    and established the law in Israel,
which he commanded our ancestors
    to teach their children,
⁶so the next generation would know them,
    even the children yet to be born,
    and they in turn would tell their children.
⁷Then they would put their trust in God
    and would not forget his deeds
    but would keep his commands.

⁸They would not be like their ancestors—
    a stubborn and rebellious generation,
whose hearts were not loyal to God,
    whose spirits were not faithful to him.

⁹The men of Ephraim, though armed with bows,
    turned back on the day of battle;
¹⁰they did not keep God's covenant
    and refused to live by his law.
¹¹They forgot what he had done,
    the wonders he had shown them.
¹²He did miracles in the sight of their ancestors
    in the land of Egypt, in the region of Zoan.
¹³He divided the sea and led them through;
    he made the water stand up like a wall.
¹⁴He guided them with the cloud by day
    and with light from the fire all night.
¹⁵He split the rocks in the wilderness
    and gave them water as abundant as the seas;
¹⁶he brought streams out of a rocky crag
    and made water flow down like rivers.

¹⁷But they continued to sin against him,
    rebelling in the wilderness against the Most High.
¹⁸They willfully put God to the test
    by demanding the food they craved.
¹⁹They spoke against God;
    they said, "Can God really
    spread a table in the wilderness?
²⁰True, he struck the rock,
    and water gushed out,
    streams flowed abundantly,
but can he also give us bread?

Can he supply meat for his people?"
[21] When the LORD heard them, he was furious;
   his fire broke out against Jacob,
   and his wrath rose against Israel,
[22] for they did not believe in God
   or trust in his deliverance.
[23] Yet he gave a command to the skies above
   and opened the doors of the heavens;
[24] he rained down manna for the people to eat,
   he gave them the grain of heaven.
[25] Human beings ate the bread of angels;
   he sent them all the food they could eat.
[26] He let loose the east wind from the heavens
   and by his power made the south wind blow.
[27] He rained meat down on them like dust,
   birds like sand on the seashore.
[28] He made them come down inside their camp,
   all around their tents.
[29] They ate till they were gorged—
   he had given them what they craved.
[30] But before they turned from what they craved,
   even while the food was still in their mouths,
[31] God's anger rose against them;
   he put to death the sturdiest among them,
   cutting down the young men of Israel.

[32] In spite of all this, they kept on sinning;
   in spite of his wonders, they did not believe.
[33] So he ended their days in futility
   and their years in terror.
[34] Whenever God slew them, they would seek him;
   they eagerly turned to him again.
[35] They remembered that God was their Rock,

that God Most High was their Redeemer.
³⁶ But then they would flatter him with their mouths,
   lying to him with their tongues;
³⁷ their hearts were not loyal to him,
   they were not faithful to his covenant.
³⁸ Yet he was merciful;
   he forgave their iniquities
   and did not destroy them.
Time after time he restrained his anger
   and did not stir up his full wrath.
³⁹ He remembered that they were but flesh,
   a passing breeze that does not return.

⁴⁰ How often they rebelled against him in the
wilderness
   and grieved him in the wasteland!
⁴¹ Again and again they put God to the test;
   they vexed the Holy One of Israel.
⁴² They did not remember his power—
   the day he redeemed them from the oppressor,
⁴³ the day he displayed his signs in Egypt,
   his wonders in the region of Zoan.
⁴⁴ He turned their river into blood;
   they could not drink from their streams.
⁴⁵ He sent swarms of flies that devoured them,
   and frogs that devastated them.
⁴⁶ He gave their crops to the grasshopper,
   their produce to the locust.
⁴⁷ He destroyed their vines with hail
   and their sycamore-figs with sleet.
⁴⁸ He gave over their cattle to the hail,
   their livestock to bolts of lightning.
⁴⁹ He unleashed against them his hot anger,

his wrath, indignation and hostility—
  a band of destroying angels.
[50] He prepared a path for his anger;
  he did not spare them from death
  but gave them over to the plague.
[51] He struck down all the firstborn of Egypt,
  the first fruits of manhood in the tents of Ham.
[52] But he brought his people out like a flock;
  he led them like sheep through the wilderness.
[53] He guided them safely, so they were unafraid;
  but the sea engulfed their enemies.
[54] And so he brought them to the border of his holy
land,
  to the hill country his right hand had taken.
[55] He drove out nations before them
  and allotted their lands to them as an inheritance;
  he settled the tribes of Israel in their homes.

[56] But they put God to the test
  and rebelled against the Most High;
  they did not keep his statutes.
[57] Like their ancestors they were disloyal and faithless,
  as unreliable as a faulty bow.
[58] They angered him with their high places;
  they aroused his jealousy with their idols.
[59] When God heard them, he was furious;
  he rejected Israel completely.
[60] He abandoned the tabernacle of Shiloh,
  the tent he had set up among humans.
[61] He sent the ark of his might into captivity,
  his splendor into the hands of the enemy.
[62] He gave his people over to the sword;
  he was furious with his inheritance.

[63] Fire consumed their young men,
    and their young women had no wedding songs;
[64] their priests were put to the sword,
    and their widows could not weep.

[65] Then the Lord awoke as from sleep,
    as a warrior wakes from the stupor of wine.
[66] He beat back his enemies;
    he put them to everlasting shame.
[67] Then he rejected the tents of Joseph,
    he did not choose the tribe of Ephraim;
[68] but he chose the tribe of Judah,
    Mount Zion, which he loved.
[69] He built his sanctuary like the heights,
    like the earth that he established forever.
[70] He chose David his servant
    and took him from the sheep pens;
[71] from tending the sheep he brought him
    to be the shepherd of his people Jacob,
    of Israel his inheritance.
[72] And David shepherded them with integrity of heart;
    with skillful hands he led them.

Carren read the last scripture and a smile covered her face. To think Asaph trusted her to tell the next generation of the praiseworthy deeds of the Lord.

She picked her bible and start reading about David who shepherded the people. As she knew David was a great warrior, a man so near to God's heart.

Please leave or share your testimonies at avrilrcordom@gmail.com

More books by the author

Action-Zbor from a mystical mountain, an Action Hero, with the speed of lightening and a sword shooting word arrows- assigned to help those in need. He has an invisible book implanted on his right arm – that gives him wisdom, knowledge and strategy.

He is a great warrior with sword, craft and speed. He outsmart the work of the mountain witch. He has two best friends at his side and two guardians watching over him. He came face to face with the evil mountain ruler, Nakonda and his cousin, Nakonda Young.

Action-Zbor has one weakness- Anger! This caused him to land in Nakonda's hands. The Pixie Guardian he once rescued, came to his rescue. The question – will she and the rest be strong enough to rescue him?

Wherever you are, **Success for the Puzzled Teenager** motivates the teen towards a higher level of personal development in this challenging world.

Teens seldom listen to adults and teachers advice of how to become their own personal successful master of life. With every chapter they are challenged to overcome their mediocrity, unlock their full potential and run a race called Success.

Testimonies at the end of each chapter, challenges teens to master whatever difficulties they are experiencing, whether the child of a single parent, sexually abused teen, alcoholic parent, loveless home, abusive relationship, divorce, shack dweller, Aids victim and the list continues. It guides them back on track to walk out as the winner who they've been created to be!

We all know how to sow, but not how to harvest. Learn how to ask your 100/60/30 fold return on your money and make it multiply. The 100/60/30 fold principle is a secret of the kingdom of heaven. If you know and apply it, you won't have lack another day in your life again.

Testimony after testimony unfolds to make you aware, why your finances are in shambles, as while you sleep, there's an enemy at work, blocking and destroying your harvest.

This step by step guide will help you restore your finances in the most simplified way. Be blessed and start multiplying your finances.